Declan

Kate Allenton

Discover other titles by Kate Allenton

At

www.kateallenton.com

ISBN-13: 978-0692529164
ISBN-10: 0692529160

ACKNOWLEDGMENTS

I'd like to acknowledge my
READERS....You all rock.
Thank you for taking a chance on my
books.

1 CHAPTER

"Who's your date to the wedding?" The bride to be, Skylar Love, asked her best friend and Maid of Honor, Olivia Parks, as they huddled in quiet conversation on the pool patio at Skylar's parents' home. Olivia knew the question was coming. Sunday lunch was part of their weekend routine and lately the time had been filled with wedding plans and preparations.

Olivia glanced toward Sky's fiancé, Luke and the brothers as they threw the football and tackled each other in the grassy back yard beyond the pool. No Sunday brunch would be complete without the guys playing the game.

Olivia cringed as she watched Flynn take an elbow to the gut as Declan shoved his way to the imaginary end zone. A tinge of sadness overcame her while watching

Declan, the oldest out of the bunch and the one she'd crushed on growing up. He wiped the sweat from his brow as he chuckled at something one of the other ones said.

Declan did his normal victory dance before holding out his hand to Flynn to pull him up from the ground. Declan was a man that got his way in everything he did, and that was one of the things she admired about him. Oliva returned her gaze to Sky, ignoring what she'd never have.

"I don't have a date, yet."

Skylar leaned in closer and whispered, "Why don't you just ask him?"

"Sky, if Declan was interested, he would have asked long before now. I'm tired of waiting for him to grow a pair of balls."

Skylar let out a full-belly laugh, tossing her head back. Olivia's cheeks heated as Sky's brothers glanced in their direction. Luke nudged Declan with his elbow, saying some words Olivia couldn't hear and then chuckled again.

"Lunch is ready. Time to come in and get cleaned up," Mary Love, Sky's mother, announced.

Luke waited on the patio as Sky and Olivia crossed the yard.

"Just remember, he'll know if you're lying," Sky whispered.

"I know. He's a human lie detector, which just makes my life more miserable," she answered as they met Luke in front of the double doors into the house.

The entire Love family had unexplainable gifts. Skylar could see colored energy-like auras around everything. Declan was like a human lie detector. Flynn had the gift of precognition, although he'd never had any visions of Olivia, at least not that he'd told her. Reed was a genius without his gift. And poor Landon, the brother that most avoided coming back home, had it the worst with the gift of enhanced senses. He'd joined the military and used his gifts during the secret missions he couldn't talk about.

"Are you talking about Declan?"

Sky stood on her tiptoes and kissed her fiancé. "Yep."

"Let me give you a little advice." He turned his gaze toward Olivia while tossing his arm over Skylar's shoulders. "Silence is the key with Declan if you don't want him knowing your secrets. If he asks, then don't answer. He won't have anything to gauge your honesty by."

Olivia mulled around that information, and her mood lightened. Luke was right. She didn't have to answer. It might not be polite, but she was past the point of being polite with the stubborn ox. She grinned.

"Thanks."

"Aw, honey, you're so sweet." Skylar rested her head on his shoulder. "I love that you gave my best friend advice to ignore my brother. I've been trying to tell her that for years."

He chuckled and led them all inside.

Luke pulled out Sky's chair and waited for her to sit before doing the same for Olivia.

"Now why can't you boys be more like Luke?" Sky's mom said while swatting Flynn and Declan with her hand towel.

Flynn, the jock of the bunch, tossed up his hands. "Dude, you're giving us a bad name. Stop doing that shit."

"Flynn." Martin Love, Sky's father's, voice boomed through the dining room. "You know better than to talk like that with ladies present."

"Sorry, Mom." Flynn leaned over and kissed his mother's cheek before taking a seat opposite Luke.

"Have you made the seating arrangements for the reception yet?" Mary asked while dishing herself a small helping of mashed potatoes.

"Not yet, but it's on my to-do list."

Luke glanced at Sky. His lips tilted at the corners. "We have a to-do list?"

"Don't worry, Luke," Olivia answered while passing the green beans. "I'm helping her tackle most of it."

"That's because you're a good best friend," Mary chimed in.

"The best," Sky added.

"So who is the lucky man coming as your date to the wedding? Is he local?"

Stick with the truth, Olivia thought to herself. Declan would be able to call her out on the lie if she said she had someone lined up. "I haven't decided."

She glanced up at Declan from beneath her lashes. His intent gaze held hers while holding his fork of roast inches from his lips. *Sorry, Dec.* She held in her smirk. There was nothing for him to decipher. His face was unreadable as if he were deliberating whether a criminal he was interrogating was lying.

"Well, I'm sure he'll be one lucky guy," Mary continued.

"Why not go stag?" Flynn asked. "That's what I'm going to do. I'm sure there will be plenty of hot chicks to choose from." His grin grew as he continued, "You know if it doesn't work out with them, I'll dance all night with you."

Declan narrowed his eyes in a scowl in Flynn's direction. "She's not like you, Flynn. She's not after a one-night stand. Are you?" He slowly turned his gaze toward Olivia.

Olivia choked on her water, covering her lips with her hands. Declan watched her, waiting for any telltale sign. One she wouldn't be giving him. Silence was golden, but how was she going to get out of blatantly ignoring his question?

"Why do you care?" Reed asked. The quieter brother spoke up. He tilted his head as if studying Declan ready to analyze his answer. "It's not like you're asking her out."

"Olivia and I are just friends."

And there was the answer to the question she'd been unable to ask and tiptoeing around her entire life. Her stomach dipped and rolled as she hid the disappointment seeping into her bones. She'd always known his answer, but hearing it out loud from the horse's mouth, well, that just sucked hairy balls. *It's official. He's a jackass.* She looked up to find Reed watching her, and a look of pity shown in his eyes. She gave him a sad smile.

Skylar pointed her fork in the air. "Who are you bringing, Reed?"

Reed sputtered. "I haven't decided."

"Like you have options," Flynn joked and knocked his brother's arm.

Thankfully the conversation moved past dates and on to more interesting aspects of the wedding like food, cake, and dresses. A hollow ache bloomed inside of Olivia as she sat quietly through the meal, watching the others while picking at her food. On more than one occasion, she'd caught Declan looking at her in silent question.

After lunch, Sky and Luke helped clean dishes.

"I'm going to head out unless you need help." Olivia spoke quietly so the others couldn't hear.

"Don't let Declan run you off," Sky answered.

"That would imply he put in effort. Which we both know isn't happening." Olivia rolled her eyes.

"Then again, if she runs, he might actually chase." Luke smiled as he wiped a plate and stuck it in the drainer.

Sky stopped washing and turned to him, her brows dipping. "We're talking about Declan. He wouldn't know a good thing if it bit him in the ass."

Luke nodded. "You've got a point." Luke gestured toward the back door. "I'd go through the backyard if you want to avoid him. I'm sure they're settled into watching sports in the living room."

"Thanks." Oliva plastered a fake smile on her face. "Call me tomorrow, Sky, and we'll do wedding stuff and check out how the rebuild of our store is going."

Thinking of the rebuild left a sour taste in Olivia's mouth. It reminded her of the maniac that had put Luke and Sky through hell. In a weeks' time he'd managed to burn down Sky and Olivia's store they'd spent their entire life planning and trying to kill Luke and Sky in the process. The killer had left Olivia fighting nightmares for months to follow.

Olivia made it home without incident and tossed her purse and keys on the foyer in the entryway. Heading straight for the kitchen, she pulled out her favorite chunky monkey ice cream and a large spoon. She needed a date. There was no way in hell she'd be showing up at the wedding without one. She just needed to find a good-looking guy to hang on his arm. That was doable. It wasn't as if she was homely. *Was she?* She pushed that thought out of her mind. She should be able to find a damn date. She gorged on the creamy goodness as she settled in for the night in front of a sappy movie, eventually letting all thoughts of Declan and his proclamation of being friends slip further from her mind. She fell asleep on the couch.

Waking the next morning, she took her time putting on her makeup and doing her hair. After slipping into a cute sundress, she grabbed her purse and headed to Sky's house. She had a new goal for the rest of the week. Finding a man was at the top of her list. Even if it wasn't the one she wanted. Declan wasn't the only fish in the sea. She just needed to change her bait.

2 CHAPTER

Olivia met Skylar at the coffee shop on Main Street only a block away from the construction site where their new shop was being built. Locals and tourists alike came through the doors looking for a jolt of caffeine before starting their days.

She watched Luke kiss Sky's cheek as he took his coffee to go. Olivia wanted a love like that. Hell, she'd just take a date for the wedding. She wasn't being picky. She left out a long sigh. "Sky?"

"Hmm?" Sky mumbled with her mouth around the coffee lid.

"Do I have loser stamped on my forehead? Why can't I get a date?"

Sky's lips twitched as she rested her cup on the table. "I wouldn't be best friends with a loser."

"Yes you would because you're nice

like that."

Sky smiled. "Well okay, I would, but you aren't a loser. You're beautiful, smart, and my best friend. There's nothing's wrong with you. If this is about Declan…"

"He's a blind ass, but this isn't just about him." She leaned forward to whisper. "I don't remember the last date I went on. It's like I checked out of my life or something."

Well, Declan was partially to blame, but in the big scheme of things, she honestly couldn't remember the last date she'd had. She'd been so busy at their collectables shop that she hadn't bothered with the opposite sex.

The bell above the door chimed before Flynn strolled in. The women in the room watched mesmerized as he moved to the counter. He was a looker. Men wanted to be him, and women just wanted an ounce of his attention. Olivia leaned across the table and lowered her voice.

"Guys don't look at me the way they look at you. Look at Flynn." Sky glanced over her shoulder before turning back.

"What about Flynn?"

"He walks into a room, and he's a chick magnet. Women watch him like they want to eat him up."

Skylar's brows dipped as she turned in her seat, scanning the room. "Flynn." She waved him over.

"Sky, don't. You'll give him an ever bigger ego." Olivia's cheeks heated.

"It's fine," she said reassuringly. "If his ego grows I'll just have to burst it. I'm really good at that." Sky grinned. "But he'll be honest with us."

Olivia's heart raced with panic as she eyed the door, wondering if she could make a run for it. Did she really want to know what guys though of her?

Flynn sauntered over to the table with a sexy smile and twinkle in his eyes. His athletic body was hard to hide beneath the sport shirt stretched across his muscled chest. His lean, strong legs were in plain view with his track shorts. There was no denying he was sexy to most ladies. But to her, he was simply Flynn. The outrageous sports and fitness fanatic who had picked on her and Sky growing up.

"Ladies."

"Pull up a seat. We need your opinion."

"No, no we don't." Olivia's eyes widened as she furiously shook her head. "I'm sure Flynn's got a million other places to be."

Flynn watched the banter before grabbing a chair from a nearby table and straddled it backward. "I've got time. What's up?"

"Olivia thinks she's a loser and men don't find her attractive. Tell her she's wrong."

"Sky..." Olivia's mouth parted.

"We need a male opinion," she said matter-of-factly. "And who better to ask than a guy you won't date?"

He flipped his gaze to Olivia. "I'm crushed."

"Stop it. We're serious." Sky smacked his arm. "If you were a guy on the street, what would you think of Olivia? Would you ask her out if you didn't know her?"

"Flynn, you don't have to answer that." She narrowed her eyes at Skylar. "You're putting him on the spot."

She shrugged. "He'll be honest. Isn't that what you want?"

"Well, yes....but..."

Flynn's brows dipped, his smile slipped as he squeezed his eyes closed and rubbed his temple.

"Is he?" Olivia asked.

Sky nodded. "Yeah. He's having a premonition."

Flynn's eyes slid open before setting his coffee on the table and stood, holding his palm out to Olivia.

"What did you see?" She asked.

"You'll have to come with me to find out. Did you still want my opinion?"

Olivia hesitated, staring at his hand. Did she want to know what he thought? His words could do more damage than good.

"Olivia?" The humor in his voice was

gone, replaced with sincerity. "I won't bite."

She slipped her fingers through his.

"We'll be back. I'm sure she'd like to do this in private."

"Take your time." Sky waved them off. "I'll be here when you get done."

Flynn kept his fingers laced with hers as he headed down the hallway that led to the back exit. Heat blossomed throughout her body. She couldn't believe she was doing this...and with him. The only thing worse would be to have Declan sizing her up. She wasn't a timid weak woman. Since when did she care what other's thought? This was ridiculous. She was being ridiculous.

He pushed out the door before releasing his hand, stopping her next to the brick building out of view of any prying eyes. The back entrance opened up to an empty street and field passed that.

Flynn lifted her arms before releasing them to fall by her side. He took his time walking a slow circle around her. His brows dipped in concentration.

"You're sizing me up like cattle," she protested.

"That's because you are. I'm getting a fresh perspective. I'm not looking at you like my sister's best friend. I'm viewing you as any man passing you on the street. Tight ass, enough for grabbing and holding on to. Nothing wrong there."

She glanced over her shoulder, watching as he did his visual perusal. He touched her arm. "Skinny arms, but no muscle, I can help you there."

"I'll show you skinny arms." She punched his shoulder as he moved in front of her and bent down, placing his palms on her thighs, feeling her legs through her dress. "You have great legs, but we're going to tone those puppies up."

"I'm not a body builder."

"I know. You've got soft curves in all the right places." He gave her sly grin and rose to meet her gaze. "But I'm going to help you. I know what you need."

"A vacation?" She smiled.

"A vacation from your reality." He smirked back.

The thought of Flynn helping her was unimaginable, but desire stirred in her belly. Not for the man but for his potential promise. She unconsciously stepped back, pressing her back against the wall. "You better not make me into a brainless Barbie."

"Would I do that?" He chuckled. His gaze dipped down to her 34C chest. He tilted his head. "Your breasts are perfect, more than a mouthful. Your lips are plump and would set any man's imagination into overdrive." He grinned rested his hand on the wall beside her head. He glanced over his shoulder before returning to look into her eyes.

"You look like the cat that ate the canary?"

"Let's just say it's time for the show. Play along and know that I don't mean anything by this."

Her brows dipped as he moved closer, his lips less than an inch from her ear. "Wait for it," he whispered.

"Flynn?" He held a sensual finger over her lips, silencing her and stealing her question.

"Shh. Three, two..." He never made it to one before he was yanked away.

"What the hell are you doing?" Declan growled deep in his throat.

It took less than a second for Olivia to figure out that this was Flynn's premonition and knew Declan was coming. What she couldn't understand was why he was playing the dirty game with his brother.

"What does it look like I'm doing, Dec?"

Declan crossed his arms over his chest and narrowed his eyes, surveying them both. "Olivia?"

Silence or the truth? Those were her only options, and she knew it. They were both watching her, waiting for her answer. "He told me I had a nice ass and great legs."

The words popped out of her mouth

before she could stop them. So what, they were true, even if she'd left out the reason why Flynn had told her those things? It had happened. Flynn tried to hide his smile as Declan frowned.

"Is that all it takes, a simple compliment from anyone?"

"I guess you'd never know. You've never had a kind word for me." And the truth of that statement aggravated her more than any game Flynn was playing with Declan. It tore at her, anger and disappointment for wasting so much time on a man that didn't care one way or the other. Olivia crossed her arms over her chest, pegging him with her glare. "What I do isn't really any of your business."

"You know she's telling the truth," Flynn said, adding more fuel to the fire. Declan ignored him.

"So it's like that?" he asked her.

She shrugged. "You and I are friends. Isn't that what you said last night?" She threw the words right back in his face. Any hope for something more was dashed with his declaration.

"Olivia." His voice softened.

She didn't wait around for him to finish his sentence. "Flynn, I'll be inside with Skylar if you want to finish our conversation."

****

Declan watched her leave before grabbing his brother and shoving him against the wall. "Why are you screwing with her?"

Flynn shoved back. "Me? You're a hypocrite, Dec." He stepped up into Declan's face. "What's the matter? You don't want her, but no one else can have her either?"

Declan stepped back as if he'd been physically punched in the gut. Olivia hadn't lied, and now, watching his brother, he knew Flynn was speaking the truth. Declan's gaze shot to the closed door before returning to his brother's glare. He unclenched his jaw and rubbed the back of his neck. "She's free to date whoever she wants."

"As long as it's not me?"

His brother wasn't stupid after all. "Yep."

Flynn's brows dipped. "Why? Give me one good reason."

"Sunday lunch would be awkward."

Flynn shook his head. "Or a hell of a lot more fun. Your reason isn't good enough, sorry, bro." Flynn yanked the door open and left Declan standing on the street.

What the hell was Flynn thinking? Olivia was setting herself up for disaster. Flynn was playing her like he had every girl he'd ever met. She didn't deserve that.

She would be crushed.

"Son of a bitch." He stormed off in the opposite direction with a headache stinging behind his eyes. Olivia deserved better. She always had. Better than Declan and most certainly better than his playboy brother. He had to stop this before anything started. The only reason he'd even been behind the building was a report of trouble making teens making that area their latest hang out. Teens weren't causing the issue today, it was his damn brother.

He turned the corner, heading back to his SUV. His mind raced with ways to stop them both.

****

Flynn stormed down the hall and back to the table and retook his seat. "I'm in. With my help, you'll be the most desired woman in town."

Sky's lips twitched. "She told me about Declan. It pissed you off, didn't it?"

"That smug son of a bitch." He leaned in and lowered his voice. "He deserves what's coming for him. We all know he's holding back, we just need to guide him to the light."

"The light being Olivia." Sky smiled.

Olivia paused with the coffee cup on her lips. "He's not holding back. You heard him at lunch."

"Oh please." Flynn waved her response away as though he hadn't heard it. "He's got it bad for you; he just won't get out of his own way. We all know it. Now it's just a matter of time to give him a good kick in the ass in the right direction."

Skylar laughed, and Olivia felt the blood drain from her face. She leaned in. "This is a bad idea. I'm not sure I want to be a part of it."

Skylar reached across the table and placed her palm over Olivia's hand. "Honey, it's time he either shits or gets off the pot. He's holding you back. Wouldn't you like to know if he's interested once and for all? If nothing more, then so you won't have any regrets. You can move on free and clear."

Olivia slid her hand free. "Not like this. Don't you think this is taking it to the extreme?"

"This is Declan we're talking about." Flynn's smile returned. "Extreme is the only way he'll see the truth." He reached for her arm and rubbed. "Don't worry, Olivia. Everything is going to be fine."

If that were the case, then why did she feel like a five-pound rock sat in the pit of her stomach? "I'm trusting you." She held Flynn's gaze. "But really this isn't about him. It's about me."

"Right." Flynn took a sip of his coffee.

"You need a date for the wedding and I'm going to help you find one." He nodded.

Flynn rose and leaned down and kissed her cheek. "I won't let him hurt you anymore." He took her hand and squeezed. "Meet me at the park at six a.m. in your jogging clothes. Operation Man Hunt has commenced."

Before she could respond, he was gone.

3 CHAPTER

Olivia woke the next morning at five thirty a.m. and cursed Operation Man Hunt. What the hell had she been thinking? She enjoyed her easy jogs, but that was as much exercise as her body was used to. She arrived at the park right on time to find Flynn waiting and his shirt already soaking with sweat.

"Did you already run? Am I late?" she asked as she approached.

"I normally do five miles, but I stopped at four so we could do the last mile or two together."

"Great." Olivia put her foot on the bench and started stretching as Flynn guzzled water from his bottle. When he was done, he wiped his lips with the back of his hand.

"So I've been thinking..."

"You ready to back out?"

"What?" He looked at her incredulously. "Not a chance. I was thinking I need to see you in action to see what I'm working with. You need some dates."

"Excuse me?" She pulled her foot behind her, stretching her hamstrings. "And where do you expect me to find a date?"

He grinned. "Leave that part up to me. For now, we run. We've gotta build up that body and stamina for the marathon sex you're going to have."

She chuckled. Flynn was crazy. She'd known that coming into it, and the fact that she was at the park this early in the morning on a Tuesday meant that she was a little crazy herself. "I've never had marathon sex. I wouldn't even know where to begin."

"Seriously?" He tisked. "That's a shame. You don't know what you're missing."

"I'll have to take your word for it."

They started out in a light jog. Flynn was a natural, whereas after a half-mile, the blood was rushing to her ears. Her lungs gasped for air when he picked up the pace after the first mile, and he pushed her to do a second. They slowed to a walk in the quarter-mile home stretch.

"Don't look now, but we have company."

She spun around to find Declan closing the distance behind them, and he passed them without a word.

"Does he always run in the park?"

"Like clockwork." Flynn's smile grew. The little shit.

"You did this on purpose?"

"Of course I did." Flynn smacked her ass. She squealed at the unexpected move. Declan was on the opposite side of the track watching them. "Come on. I'll race you to the bench. Loser buys coffee."

"You're on." She took off faster than she knew her feet could carry her. He beat her to the bench by a landslide.

The coffee shop filled as customers came and went as they sat at a window table. Flynn was oblivious to the stares they garnered, but she wasn't. The women in the place were jealous he was with her and not with them. His easy banter and carefree attitude drew her attention back to him and away from the onlookers. When he pulled out his cell and arranged a date for her, coffee spewed from her lips.

He grinned as he watched her while talking quietly into the phone. "Tonight at seven. I'll give you the directions."

He hung up and eased back in his

chair as if he'd just won a prize.

"Tell me you didn't."

"Of course I did. Paul Marks will pick you up at eight."

"Why?"

"Why the date? We've already discussed this. I need to see you in action."

A blind date already made her uneasy, but having Flynn tag along made her mortified. "You're coming with us?"

"No, but I'll be nearby." He smiled.

She knew everyone on the island and had grown up with most of the people who lived there, and yet, Paul's name didn't ring any bells. "Who's Paul Marks? He can't be local. I've never met him."

"He's a friend." Flynn leaned closer. "And don't worry."

Words to live by. If she didn't worry, then who would? She was going out with a stranger.

****

After spending the day with her stomach in knots, she showered and changed in record time. Her doorbell rang at six o'clock. She answered the door to find Flynn on her stoop. "What are you doing here?"

"Making sure you're prepared." He gave a slow perusal down her body and back up. She fidgeted in her dress pants and silk shirt. "This won't do." He turned and waved to the car. His cousin Alexis stepped out, carrying a large container, and walked up the sidewalk.

"Olivia, you know Alexis."

"Hi," she answered as Flynn and Alexis pushed their way into her house. "Okay," she mumbled beneath her breath.

Alexis and Flynn disappeared toward her bedroom, and she was left to follow.

Flynn was in her closet, sifting through her hangers. He pulled out the only black cocktail dress she owned and grabbed the matching three-inch heels and tossed them onto the bed. "Wear that."

He walked out of the room as Alexis poked her head out of the bathroom. "Get your cute butt in here. I only have two hours to make you into a goddess that all men will worship."

Olivia glanced at the makeup box taking up all the space on her bathroom counter. "Cute...I'd agree with, but...goddess. I think your expectations are too high."

"We both know you've already nailed the girl-next-door look. We're just upping the ante."

Alexis took Olivia's arms and eased her to sit on the toilet. "If you don't like it, you can remove it."

Olivia sat quietly while Alexis took her time working on Olivia's makeup. Alexis worried her bottom lip and tilted her head as she stared at Olivia's face as if it were a canvas to be decorated.

"This may be a shock if you aren't used to wearing this much makeup, but I was right. You're a knockout." She gestured to the mirror. "Take a look."

Olivia rose and moved to the mirror. Her mouth parted as she stared at her smoky eyes. The black and grays on her lids and eyelashes made her blue eyes appear sultry and sexy. Her red lips were finished in an easy gloss. "How did you do that?"

"The makeup was a piece of cake since I already had a great canvas to start with. So adding a few mere touches only brought out the great assets you already had."

Olivia lifted her hand to her stomach and leaned in closer. "Damn your good."

Alexis glanced at her watch. "You need to change, or you won't be ready before he gets here."

Alexis gathered her things and left Olivia to change into the slinky dress. The black material slid over her curves, cupping her in all the right places. She took her time and pinned her hair up into a messy, yet sexy, updo with a few strands framing her face before slipping into her heels. One final look in the full-length mirror on the back of the door and she barely recognized the woman staring back at her. Was this the kind of woman that Declan wanted?

"Let us see," Flynn called from the living room.

She let out a final sigh and left the security of her bedroom. Flynn's eyes lit up when she stood in front of them and did a slow spin in place.

"Do you approve?'

"Fuck yeah."

"You kiss your momma with that mouth?" Alexis smacked his stomach.

Flynn ignored her. His gaze started at her head and moved slowly down her body. "If you weren't my brother's girl, I might have to make a play."

She waved off the comment. "I'm not your brother's girl."

"That's right. She's her own woman." Alexis slowly rounded Olivia and smiled. "You're confidence makes you sexy."

"Damn right," Flynn added before glancing at his watch. "Her strength is probably why Declan never made a move. Too worried he'd get shot down."

Olivia busted out laughing.

Flynn winked. "We need to leave before Paul gets here."

Olivia saw them out and closed the door and had moved back into her room to grab a black clutch that matched her dress when she heard a knock on the door.

A quick glance at the bedside clock, and her brows dipped. "He's ten minutes early." She inhaled a quick breath and tossed her cell and wallet in the clutch then went to the door. Pasting a smile on her face, she pulled the door open.

Expecting to meet Paul, she came face to face with Declan. He took his time running his gaze down her body and back up. "What did you do?"

Olivia crossed her arms over her chest, and Declan's gaze zeroed in on her breasts. "What are you doing here?"

He stepped around her and into the house.

"Do all of you Loves just barge in?"

Declan ignored her comment and waited for her to close the door. "You can't date Flynn," he growled scanning her dress again.

This was an unexpected surprise. Had he finally come to his senses and figured things out? "Why not?"

"You two won't ever work."

Any hope she'd been feeling was squished just like a damn bug on the windshield of her life. She let out an exasperated sigh. "Why? He's sexy, smart, has a great body and a fun personality. He's the type of guy any woman would want."

Declan advanced on her quicker than she'd ever seen him move. She took an unconscious step back, the door stopping her retreat. His palms rested on the door on both sides of her head, caging her like an animal. Her heartbeat doubled, dancing in her chest.

"You're too good for him." His gaze searched hers, his brown eyes reading clear to her soul. His gaze dropped to her lips. An inch separated them. One small move and she could claim his lips and finally know what it felt like to kiss him.

She swallowed around the lump in her throat. She hesitated on how much to tell him, hell, what to tell him. "Declan..."

"Call off your date with Flynn," he demanded pulling her out of her lust-filled haze. The butterflies in her belly quieted, replaced with disappointment. He'd had his moment. He could have done anything, said anything, other than make a demand, and she might have listened.

"I don't have a date with Flynn." She pushed against his chest, reclaiming her space and her sanity. "I have a date with Paul Marks."

As if right on cue, her doorbell rang, and she pulled it open and smiled. The guy standing outside held a bouquet of roses. His dark gray charcoal suit was custom-made, hugging him in all the right places. His black hair and dark eyes made him look like a mystery, which, when she thought about it, he really was.

"Paul." She smiled. "You're right on time." She stepped back and let him in.

Paul spotted Declan and turned to her. "Am I interrupting?"

Declan was quick to answer. "Yes."

"No," she contradicted and held the door open. "Declan's a friend, and he was just leaving."

Declan grunted and walked to the door. He gave a quick glance over his shoulder before holding her gaze. "This conversation isn't over."

She smiled. "Yes, it is."

He walked out, and she closed the door. Alone with a stranger in her house. Not the best idea she'd ever had, but Flynn trusted the guy.

He held out the bouquet. "These are for you."

"Thank you. Let me just put them in water and we can leave." She graciously accepted them before walking into the kitchen and putting them in a vase. She sniffed the roses, letting the lovely scent fill her nostrils and calm her nerves before walking back into the living room.

"Are you ready?"

She smiled and grabbed her purse. "More than ever."

4 CHAPTER

Declan grumbled all the way to the car while clenching his fist. Seeing this new jackass show up, he'd wanted to grab him by the scruff of his neck and toss his bony ass out into the lawn. What the hell was she thinking? Olivia didn't date, and yet she was dressed for sin and going out with some prick that Declan didn't know a damn thing about. He slipped his phone out of his pocket and punched the familiar numbers before sticking it to his ear.

"I need a background check on Paul Marks, address unknown, height over six feet, dark hair, dark eyes. I need it ASAP."

"Sure thing, boss," the deputy on the other end agreed before Declan disconnected the call.

Technically he got what he came to her house for. She wasn't going on a date with Flynn but with another guy. He hadn't expected the twist of events. He slid into the SUV and clutched the steering wheel while moving his vehicle to a side road. Someone had to watch out for her, damn it, and if Sky and Flynn wouldn't, then he damn sure would.

He called Skylar next. When he got her voicemail, he cursed before dialing Flynn. His brother picked up on the first ring.

"What's up?"

"Don't what's up me. You know damn good and well. I saw you leaving her house."

Flynn chuckled. "Don't tell me you've turned into a stalker."

"What? No." Declan's face heated. "I went over there to talk some sense into her."

"Yeah? How did that work out for you?"

Declan rubbed the ache in his chest as he watched the pair through his rearview mirror get into a car and pull out. "She blew me off. She's got a damn date tonight."

Flynn's raucous laughter turned louder, and Declan held the phone away from his ear until the laughter receded.

"Good for her." Declan could hear the humor in Flynn's voice. "I bet she'll get lucky tonight. It's high time someone tapped that ass."

"Flynn," Declan growled. "No one is tapping anything." Declan heard people talking and glasses clinking in the background. "Where are you?"

"LaAmour having a beer. Why don't you come join me, and you can drown your sorrows at losing the best thing that ever happened to you."

"Fuck you."

"I guess you met Paul."

"How do you know his name?"

"I set her up. Did you know she's never had marathon sex?" Flynn paused. "I was thinking he could be our third, and we could make all of her dreams come true."

"Over my dead body." Declan hung up and gassed the pedal, sending pebbles on the road flying as white smoke peeled from his tires. He was going to kill Flynn. Olivia was headed for disaster, and Flynn's games ended tonight, one way or another, even if he had to beat his brother and Olivia's date to a pulp. Neither one of them were touching her.

Declan pulled up outside the restaurant and immediately spotted Paul's car. His phone rang.

"Boss, Paul Marsh is a male escort from the mainland."

"Thanks." Declan hung up and sat in his car, mulling around the new information. Did Olivia know? Hell, had Flynn hired him?

Declan opened the door and spotted Flynn at the bar, only pausing when he noticed Skylar sitting next to him, sipping a glass of wine. He followed their gaze to a table in the restaurant where Olivia was sitting with her date. She glowed. A smile lit her face as she talked to the stranger. She chuckled at something he said, and he laid his palm over her hand. A blush crossed her cheeks. He could hardly tear his eyes away from watching her. He thought she was already beautiful, but seeing her face light up from the words of another man felt like a vise grip tightening around his heart.

Sky wrapped her palm around Declan's bicep. "Staring is rude." She chuckled. "Come sit with us. We have a great view."

To avoid strangling Flynn, he took the seat on the opposite side of Skylar. The bartender brought over a beer and placed it on a napkin in front of him. He didn't question how the bartender knew. Declan was too busy watching Olivia across the room.

"She won't appreciate that you're here," Sky whispered, lifting the wine glass to her lips and sipping.

"Someone has to protect her," he answered.

Flynn leaned across the bar to see Declan. "Maybe she doesn't want a protector. Maybe she's tired of being coddled and needs a real man that's ready to step up to the plate."

Declan's blood curdled, and his grip on the beer bottle tightened. "So you think a male escort can do the trick?"

Flynn tossed his head back and laughed. "You did a background check on her date?

"She's going to love that." Sky grinned.

"You've got it worse than I thought." Flynn rose from his seat and stood next to his brother, draping his arm over his shoulder. "Look at her." They both looked in the couple's direction again. "She could have any man in this place falling at her feet."

Olivia sensually crossed her legs and dabbled a napkin at her red pouty lips. She was sex on a stick, and his jeans tightened in response. One look when she'd opened the door earlier and he'd refrained from reaching for her. When he'd backed her up against the door, it had about killed him not to kiss and claim her. Declan rubbed his hand over his face.

"She deserves better. Something real and lasting."

"You're right," Flynn answered. "And if she wasn't totally in love with you, I'd be the one giving it to her."

Declan snapped his gaze to his brother. "She doesn't love me." He pointed to Olivia's table. "Look at her. Does that look like a woman in love?"

Sky turned to face him. "Declan, how I see it is you have two choices but time is running out."

He glanced at his sister.

"She wants more, and I can't say I blame her. Every girl wants to be loved, and it sucks when the person you love doesn't realize it. I should know, but at least in my case, Luke was smart enough to figure it out. Now you, on the other hand, needed a good kick in the ass, and that's what Flynn gave you. So you have an option. You can either man up and take a risk and see how things work out, or she could find what she's looking for in the arms of another man."

Declan's mouth parted before he snapped it shut and turned to Flynn. "You did all of this as a game?"

"No." Flynn's jovial manner sobered. "I did all of this because you're my brother and I only ever wanted what's best for you...and her. Now quit being a putz before you lose her for good. It's time."

He returned his gaze to Olivia's table to find that she was staring at him. He caught a glimpse of the sadness in her eyes before she masked it and looked away. She dabbed her lips and spoke in hushed tones before she stood and headed toward the bathroom hallway.

****

Paul was a nice guy, even great looking. He'd caught several eyes when they walked into the restaurant. Yet, he wasn't Declan. Talking with Paul, she'd come clean, telling him her heart wasn't in it and apologized. When he'd smiled and reached for her hand, he'd told her he was having a good time and to relax.

Olivia walked into the bathroom and straight to the mirror. Her breath came out raggedly as she stared at her reflection. Why was Declan here? She'd seen Sky and Flynn, knew they were watching her, but why Declan? Had he come to watch her fall flat on her face during her date? She closed her eyes as her cheeks heated.

The door behind her creaked, and she opened her eyes to find Declan standing on the threshold. He stepped inside and closed the door, flicking the lock.

Confusion clouded her mind as she spun around. "What are you doing here?" she asked softly. Any fight she'd had earlier fled her body.

Declan kept his distance between them. "I came to beat up Flynn."

She closed her eyes and dropped her

gaze, shaking her head. "Flynn was just trying to help." She lifted her head. "Why are you in the bathroom?"

He answered without hesitation. "I followed you. I saw my opportunity, and I took it."

He closed the distance between them and rested his hand on her cheek. The butterflies in her stomach woke to his touch, flittering. Her body vibrated in apprehension. "Dec..."

"I'm giving you what you wanted."

He lowered his head and pressed his mouth to hers. His warm lips stole her breath as he pulled her closer, tilting his head, deepening his kiss. She fell into his trance as he devoured her mouth, tasting and touching, savoring the desire only his touch could give her. His palm lay splayed on her back, possessively holding her like she'd always longed for.

When he broke the kiss, he rested his head against hers. "Is that what you wanted? Is that why you're with a male escort?"

What she wanted? Male escort? She stepped out of his hold. Fury coursed through her body when her palm connected hard with his face. Her palm stung as she held it to her chest.

"Why did you do that? So I wouldn't go home with him?" For the first time in her life, Declan had become the asshole the others had tried to warn her about. The uncaring bastard knew she had feelings, yet he was screwing with her. "Go to hell, Declan."

She stormed out of the bathroom, exchanged a few words with Paul, and grabbed her clutch. He was quick to drop bills on the table and follow her out of the restaurant.

****

Declan returned to find his siblings both scowling in his direction as he crossed the restaurant and retook his seat at the bar. He drank the whole beer, ignoring their questions until he was done.

"What the hell did you do?" Sky asked him.

"I kissed her and asked if that was what she wanted and why she was with a male escort."

Flynn tossed his arms up. "You're an idiot. No wonder she stormed out of here."

Sky reached for his red face to touch it, and he turned his head. "Looks like she got her point across."

"She thinks *I'm* the one playing games." He pointed an accusing finger toward the door. "She's the one dressed up like she's looking for action and flirting with an asshole she doesn't even know for cripes sake."

"I don't know what she sees in you, Declan." Flynn's tone was angry as he shook his head. He turned to Sky. "She wasn't the one who needed help. Declan's the one who needs to get a damn clue."

Flynn tossed some bills on the bar and stormed out of the restaurant, leaving Sky and Declan alone. Sky cleared her throat in the awkward silence between them. The last thing he wanted was to have a relationship conversation with his baby sister. Skylar spun on the stool.

"Declan, after years of ignoring her, you can't just act like a caveman and accuse her of things and expect her to fall at your feet. It doesn't work that way. She needs to feel cherished, wined and dined, and feel the excitement that a new relationship brings."

Declan grunted and lifted his hand to order another beer. He waited while the bartender flicked off the top and then drank half before answering his sister. "Sky, this is me."

"No it's not." She gave him a sad smile. "You're the guy that likes to tease her just to see her smile. You're the guy that went out of your way to make sure she stayed safe when at the hospital when the psycho was running around town. You're that guy, not this caveman you're portraying."

"I'm not the one trying to be someone I'm not. She is. I liked the old her, not this new sex-kitten version."

Skylar laid her palm on his arm. "Do you know why she wants to change?" Skylar slid off the stool and laid some bills on the bar. "She wants to be happy. She wants the white picket fence and the 2.5 kids. And I'm sure, in the back of her mind, she hopes that you'd want it to. She's at the breaking point, Dec. She's ready to give up on the only man who mattered to her and settle for someone else. Is that what you want for her? Because, to be honest, at this point, I just want her happy." She pointed to the red spot on his cheek. "And right now, you haven't convinced me, or her, that you're capable of giving her that."

Skylar kissed his cheek and left Declan sipping his beer. Her words were hard to hear, but he knew she was telling the truth. The thought of Olivia with someone else made his gut clench. Watching her enjoy herself with the guy had driven in the nail and opened his eyes. He'd wasted years working on his career and keeping any type of relationships at a distance.

5 CHAPTER

Declan woke early to get his morning jog in at the park. After a night like last night, he had energy and aggravation to burn. He jogged into the park entrance and kept running, not even stopping to stretch. He pumped his arms at his sides as his breath came out in pants. He enjoyed jogging as a simple way to relieve his stress. He replayed the scenes from last night, the way she'd looked and the asshole with her. Would he have changed anything? Hell yeah, she wouldn't have gone out on the date to begin with.

His lungs burned as he pushed harder for another mile as he remembered the look on her face when he'd kissed her. The hot, passionate kiss he'd been waiting for, yet he'd never imagined the slap she'd lain on his cheek right after. Did he deserve it? Absolutely. When it came to the Love men charming women, Flynn had been the only one to inherit that gene, but that wouldn't stop him from going after what he wanted. And until last night, it had been only heated glances from across the table and noticing the blush of her cheeks when she was embarrassed, and damned if he didn't notice the way she nibbled her bottom lip when she was nervous. He was the man who noticed those things, not the escort from last night, or even Flynn. It was Declan she belonged with, and now he just had to prove it. He'd kept her at arm's length long enough. It was time he pulled her in before someone else cut the connection for good.

Declan jogged out of the park and headed to his house. If he was going to win her over, he was going to need to apologize the best way he knew how.

****

Declan grabbed the coffees and bakery bag from his car and walked up the sidewalk to Olivia's door. After a long night of drinking and thinking, he owed her an apology, if not a hell of a lot more. As he was reaching for the doorbell, the door opened. Olivia was dressed in a sundress, her hair twisted up on her head, and her makeup just the way he liked it, understated in the girl-next-door kind of way.

"This look suits you."

"I didn't ask for your opinion." Olivia rolled her eyes and let out a long sigh. "Why are you here?"

"I wanted to apologize for last night."

"Good." She pulled the door open and let him in masking the hesitation in her eyes. "I have to leave in a few minutes."

He handed her the bakery bag. "Peace offering. It's your favorite."

She opened it and sniffed the contents. Her favorite blueberry muffins filled the bag. "How did you know?"

"I pay attention," he said, walking past her.

"That's debatable," she mumbled and shut the door.

He put the container down on the table with the coffee and turned to her, hesitating with his words. "I don't want things to be awkward."

Olivia set the bag down next to the coffee. "Nothing's changed," she reassured him. "That one kiss....meant nothing."

Lie. His lips twitched. "Everything's changed." He cleared his throat and slid his hands in his pocket. "Olivia...I need you to understand something."

Olivia crossed her arms over her chest and lifted a brow. "Oh?"

"Last night, the kiss, seeing you with someone else, it did something to me. Something I wasn't prepared for." He slid his hands out of his pocket. His heart beat heavily in his chest as he cleared his throat. "I don't know what this pull is between us, but I'm done fighting it."

She held up her hand, stopping him. "Let me save you the breath. Declan, I know you don't do relationships. I've liked you for a long time, and you were right when you said we were friends. I've always wanted more, dreamed of it actually. Then I went along with Flynn and pretended I was something more than I was. So, if what you want is the woman you saw last night, that isn't me. That will never be me, and I'm good with that. Actually great with that. There's only one thing that I've been waiting for…"

"Olivia…"

She closed the distance between them pressing her lips to his, catching him off guard. The muscles in his shoulders clenched as she held on to his hips.

He drew her body flush with his, letting her feel how much he wanted her. His hand tangled in her strands, tilting her head for better access as his tongue plundered her mouth, tasting everything she was. Her fast heartbeat matched his as her body relaxed into his, leaning into his embrace. In that minute, he knew. He broke the kiss and held her gaze. Her cheeks flushed a rosy pink, and her bruised lips parted.

"That passion isn't something that can be faked." His gaze landed on her lips as he debated taking her again. "But I...can't promise you forever."

"I don't want your promises." She pressed her lips to his. Her fingers fumbled with the button on his jeans before lowering the zipper. Her fingers slid inside, and she held him.

He groaned and held her wrist. "Olivia, don't start something you aren't prepared to finish."

"Have you ever known me to quit anything?"

Truth.

"No." He hesitated a mere second before reaching for the hem of her dress, slowly lifting it up her thighs. Her warm, long legs beckoned for attention as his fingers skimmed over her silky skin. He pulled the dress over her head and let it slip from his fingers. He held her breast, kneading it as his finger slipped below the bra and he lowered the offending fabric out of the way.

"Beautiful," he murmured as he lowered his head and sucked the plump flesh into his mouth.

He pressed his hips into hers, letting her feel exactly what she did to him.

Declan kissed a slow, sensual path up her chest to her neck, her pulse quickened beneath his lips. "Declan. I need you."

Truth.

He lifted her by the ass, and she circled her legs around him. He carried her down the hall and kicked her door closed with his foot. When his knees touched the bed, he eased her down, following her up the bed. He took his time, pressing kisses to belly as he pulled her panties off. Running his palms up and down her thighs, he spread her and licked his lips before kissing a path up to her core. He watched her face as he licked her, tasting her on his tongue delved in for the first time. Her eyes slid closed on a moan.

He spread her legs wider and kept tasting her. Sliding a finger into her tight channel, he worked it in and out, moving her closer to the edge, where he was hanging by a thread.

He slid off the bed, stepping out of his jeans and boxers. She watched him from under her heavy lids as she moved to unhook her bra. She tossed it on the floor. Her chest rose and fell in anticipation.

He pulled a condom out of his pocket and tore into the wrapper, slowly rolling it down his engorged shaft. Olivia licked her lips, her cheeks flushed as he crawled up her body and settled between her thighs. He rubbed his shaft through her juices before sliding in an inch.

"You're tight."

She swallowed. "Declan, there's something I need to tell you…"

He slid in another inch before breaching her barrier. He held himself still as he searched her eyes. "You're a virgin."

Her cheeks flushed as she nodded in answer, as if unable to speak.

Declan kissed her, leaving her breathless before moving down her chest and taking one breast in his mouth and cupping the other with his hand, increasing her pleasure to remove the upcoming pain from claiming her virginity. He scraped his teeth against her nipple before smoothing the sting with his tongue. He tweaked her nipple between his finger, and he could feel her tighten more.

He moved up to her mouth and kissed her again. "This may hurt a little."

"If you don't start moving, I may hurt you."

She lifted her hips in invitation, and he slid in farther, breaching her barrier until he was seated to the hilt. He stilled, letting her get accustomed to his size. When her body relaxed, he began to move, holding his own desire until he felt her walls clenching him.

"Oh God." She moaned, digging her nails dug into his back.

He quickened his pace. "Come for me, Olivia."

He worked her, sliding in and out, over and over until she screamed his name.

Hearing his name on her lips was his undoing. His restraint broke, shooting his seed into the latex. He stayed inside of her while he pressed his lips to hers in a lazy kiss between lovers. Panic took hold when he felt something wrong. He pulled out of her and glanced between their bodies. What should have been a full condom was empty.

He rested his head on her belly and closed his eyes, unsure how to tell her what had happened. Her fingers played in his hair. "Olivia."

"Yeah?"

He looked up at her and went with pure honesty, unable to find an easy way to tell her. "The condom broke."

She lifted up on her elbows. Panic stretched across her face. "What?"

"I'm so sorry." He climbed off the bed and went into the bathroom and discarded the condom and cleaned up before returning to clean her up. When he was done, he lay down beside her and pulled her close. "If you end up pregnant, we'll deal with it." He kissed her forehead. "I'm sorry this tainted your first time."

She leaned up on her elbow, resting her cheek in her hand. "None of what happened was tainted. It was better than I could have imagined."

Truth.

Change was needed, but it wasn't Olivia that needed to change. No, it was Declan. If anyone needed to change it was him. He needed to be the man she wanted, the one she'd dreamed of, and the one she could fall for and in order to do that, he was going to have to put in the effort. Not just a quick roll in the sack, no matter how great it was.

He released some of the tension in his muscles and stroked her arm. "You want to do dinner some time?"

Olivia rested her arm and her chin on his chest, looking up at him. "I'll think about it."

He rolled on top of her and settled between her thighs. "You're lucky I only had the one condom, or I'd make love to you again until you said yes."

She reached over to the bedside table and pulled out a new box before tossing it back inside. "As tempting as that sounds, I'm afraid I can't. I'm going to be late if I don't get cleaned up."

He pressed a kiss to her neck. "You sure your plans can't wait?"

She pressed against his shoulder, stopping his kisses. "I'm afraid not. Sky

Alexis and I are expected for our last fitting. I kind of have to be there, being the maid of honor and all. It's my duty."

"Shit." Declan glanced at the clock. "I'll drive you. I have to get fitted for my tux next door." He didn't move to get off of her. "Say yes to a date, and I'll let you go."

She hesitated, chewing her bottom lip before nodding. "Okay."

He pressed a fast kiss to her lips. "How about tonight?

She shook her head. "I can't. I have plans."

His brows dipped. "Tomorrow?"

She shrugged. "Maybe."

6 CHAPTER

Declan drove her to the shop and parked outside. He walked her to the door, pulling her to a stop and laying a kiss on her that left her dazed and giddy. He tapped her ass and opened the door for her. "Have fun."

Olivia spotted Skylar and her cousin, Alexis, in the back of the store. They waved as she approached.

"My, my, you're glowing." Alexis teased. "Did you get lucky last night?"

"Don't be ridiculous." Sky knocked her shoulder until she looked at Olivia. "Oh my god you did." She pulled Alexis and Olivia away from the seamstress. "How was it? Who was it? I need details. I really hope it didn't hurt. Was he special? I thought you were going to wait."

"Take a breath, Sky." Olivia's cheeks heated as she pulled them even farther away to the sitting area. "It wasn't last night." She couldn't contain her smile. "It was about an hour ago, and it was with....Declan."

Alexis squealed, and Sky jumped up from her seat. "Tell me he didn't." She planted her hands on her hips. "Did you tell him you were a virgin?" she demanded. "That sorry SOB hasn't even taken you on a date and he seduced you? I'll kill him."

Alexis's squeal stopped. "Wait? You're a virgin?"

"Was," she clarified before returning her gaze to Sky. "And he didn't seduce me. I seduced him when he showed up on my doorstep to apologize for being an ass last night."

Sky's jaw dropped. Words eluded her before she nodded. "Well, good for you. It's about damn time you got what you wanted. Are you dating now, or did he run scared?"

"He informed me he didn't do relationships but then asked me to dinner."

"So where is he taking you?"

Olivia rubbed her fingers together. "I told him I have plans."

Alexis's mouth parted, and Skylar grinned. "And he bought that?"

She shrugged. "It was the truth. I'd planned to go see a movie."

"I don't understand. I thought this was what you wanted."

Olivia moved to sit down on the carpeted bench in the dressing room. "He's not ready. I didn't want him to feel obligated because we had sex, and had I said yes, then I'd never know if he'd really wanted to." She held Sky's gaze. "I knew I wanted him to be my first, so I didn't think, just acted."

****

Declan sauntered into the tuxedo shop. A tailor had a measuring tape around Flynn's neck, and last night he would have used that position to strangle the bastard.

"You're late," Flynn announced. "You still licking your wounds?"

Luke, glanced Declan's way. "I heard what happened."

Declan moved into Flynn's face. "She's off the market. Do you understand?"

Flynn's lips tilted up in a cocky smirk. "That's for her to decide, bro."

Declan shook his head. "Cut the crap, Flynn. No more setting her up."

Flynn shrugged. "You aren't her

keeper. You aren't dating her. There's no reason she should sit at home every night. We both know she deserves better."

Declan tilted his head. "If I didn't know better, I'd think *you* liked her."

Flynn shrugged, and Declan lunged for his brother, but Luke pulled him back. "This isn't a game, Flynn. Back the fuck off."

"Gentleman." The tailor tisked. "The knock-down, drag-out will have to wait until after your measurements."

Flynn held up his hands in surrender.

Luke clapped Declan's back. "He's screwing with you. We both know he'll never settle down."

"Hey...." Flynn grumbled. "I can settle down if I wanted to. I just don't want to."

"I can't wait to see the day a woman brings you to your knees and the table is flipped." Luke kidded. "So have you asked her out?"

"Yeah, but she said she had plans."

"She didn't say yes?"

"No, so who's the dick you lined up for tonight?"

Flynn shook his head, walking away from the tailor. "I didn't set up a date for her tonight. Olivia deserves to be swept off her feet and cherished. I haven't found the right guy yet. Last night was just a test drive to see how she handles herself. She's a virgin, you know."

"How in the hell did you know that?" Declan grabbed Flynn's shirt.

"I could tell." Flynn brushed his brother's hands off of him. "You didn't know?"

Declan's jaw ticked, and Flynn's eyes widened as if he were peering down into Declan's soul and knew first-hand that he'd slept with her. "Tell me you didn't."

"It's none of your damn business."

Flynn threw his hands up and turned. "You deflowered her." He spun back around. "When? It wasn't last night. I checked on her after she left."

The tailor moved to Declan and started his measurements, keeping him immobile.

"Like I said, it's none of your damn business."

Flynn ran his hand through his hair. "This is my fault."

Declan's jaw ticked. "Why did you have to try and change her into a female version of you?"

"I just wanted her to be happy." Flynn's shoulders eased.

Fifteen minutes later ,after all of the alterations were complete. Luke twirled his car keys on his finger and headed to the door. "Come on, boys. Lunch is on me. I'm sure Declan's a little rusty when it comes to sweeping women off their feet."

"Bite me," he growled.

Flynn patted Declan on the back and

steered him to the door. "You need all the help you can get."

"Like you helped Olivia? No thanks. I think I can manage."

****

Sky and Olivia walked through the resort and into the pool area to look down on the beach below, where the wedding was going to be held. They were headed to LaAmour for a food tasting to approve the final touches on the reception and the cake. They both stared out into the blue water, watching the waves roll onto the beach.

"Take your time with him." Sky turned to her. "He made you wait forever; maybe it will do him some good to see you aren't pining away for him."

Olivia nodded and let out a long breath. "I want the whole package with him, not just the crumbs he's throwing my way."

Sky's phone rang, interrupting their conversation. Her eyes widened, and she gasped. "No. Oh please tell me you're joking."

"What?" Olivia turned her worried gaze on Sky, watching helplessly as the color drained from her friend's cheeks.

"I'll be right there." She slid the phone into her pocket. "They ruined my dress."

Olivia gasped. "We should leave."

Sky rested her hand on Olivia's. "The tasting, they've already prepared everything. Do you mind staying? I've already tasted the food and picked it out. This is just the final approval. Do you mind?"

"Not at all. Go...take care of the dress."

"Thank you, thank you, thank you."

Olivia walked Skylar to the parking lot before heading inside LaAmour. The normally quiet restaurant was buzzing with conversation and filled with nothing but men. She stood frozen just inside the door, her eyes scanning for anyone she knew. Skylar's father stepped out of the backroom and greeted her.

"Where's Skylar?"

"Something happened to her dress. So I'm stuck handling the food."

He nodded and showed her to a table in the bar area. "The caterers are already here preparing in the back."

"Who are all these people? You aren't normally open for lunch."

Her dad glanced behind him and grinned. "They're all here for Flynn's corporate team-building conference."

"His what?"

"Flynn organizes most of our parties and corporate conferences, specializing in team building. These guys are his group." He turned back to her. "Lunch was part of the package deal. Had I known he'd scheduled football players with healthy appetites for a two-week stint, I would have had him double the cost. Let me tell the caterers in the back that you're here, and they'll start bringing out the food and the champagne."

"Thanks." She placed her napkin on her lap and scanned the crowd of men as they talked and carried on. Several were looking her way. One specifically stood out. She'd seen his face, knew his name from watching football on Sundays with Sky's brothers. "Trent Stewart."

He held her gaze. A smile slipped onto his lips, and he gave her a slight nod. She felt the blood rushing to her cheeks and glanced away as the waiter headed in her direction with the first plate. He laid it in front of her and lifted the lid. Another server followed behind him with a bottle of champagne sitting in a bucket of ice.

"I hope you're hungry. There is a feast worthy of any palate in the kitchen."

"Perfect. Thank you." Olivia was glad she'd skipped the muffins earlier that Declan had brought. If she'd eaten them, there was no way she could eat the amount of food that she knew was coming next.

Olivia rose, grabbed the champagne bottle, and tore off the wrapper from around the cork. She tried to pry it free, worried that the cork would shoot across the room if she pressed too hard. The last think Sky's folks needed was a negligence lawsuit filed because she'd knocked a player in the head.

"Let me," a smooth voice said from behind her. His large hands slid on top of hers, taking the bottle from her hand. She turned to find Trent standing behind her, a smile curving his mouth.

"Thank you."

He worked his magic on the cork without sending anyone to the hospital and poured her a glass. "Why are you eating alone?"

His question caught her off guard. "I'm doing the food tasting for a wedding reception."

"A wedding reception. Now that makes perfect sense. I was wondering why such a beautiful woman was eating alone. When is your big day, and where's the lucky man? Shouldn't he be helping you?"

Heat crept up into Olivia's cheeks. "Oh no. This isn't my wedding. It's for my best friend, actually. She's getting married next weekend. She was here but had to leave. Some type of dress emergency."

"Oh yes, I hear dress emergencies can be brutal."

Olivia smiled and retook her seat. "So, do you have first-hand knowledge?"

"Is that your way of asking me if I'm

single?" he teased and set the champagne bottle in the ice bucket.

Olivia's mouth parted. "No, no, I didn't mean it like that."

"I'm teasing." He gave her a thousand-watt smile. "Do you care if I join you? I hate to see a woman eating alone."

Her eyes widened, and she glanced at the kitchen door. "Uh...no, I don't mind." She leaned across the table. "Maybe the others will quit looking at me."

He glanced over his shoulder before turning back to face her. "Not a chance. They're probably just pissed I talked to you first." He held up his finger. "Let me grab my plate." He grabbed his plate from his table and returned to hers. She gestured to the champagne. "Please have a glass. I'm not going to be able to drink the bottle."

He poured a glass. "So, where's your boyfriend?"

"Are you always this direct?" she asked and then took a bite of her salad.

"Yes, and you're avoiding the question."

She gave a slow nod. "Well, if you must know, I don't have one. There is someone special, but he's..."

"Got commitment issues?"

She grinned. "You must be a mind reader."

He shook his head and cut into his

steak as her salad was removed and replaced with another dish. He waited until the waiter left before answering.

"Nope, not a mind reader, but I have a sister, and I know the pensive look that just crossed your face." He lifted his glass to her in a toast. "Here's to getting everything you want."

She smiled. "Thanks, you too."

They each sipped. She was just putting her glass back on the table when Declan walked in, carrying a crate with champagne inside. He caught her gaze before narrowing his eyes on Trent.

"By the looks of it, I'd guess that's him."

"How can you tell?" she whispered.

"He looks ready to kill me."

Declan set the champagne on the bar before stomping over to their table. "Is he the reason you have plans tonight?"

Olivia felt the blood drain from her face. Trent stood, tossing his napkin on the table. "You've got this all wrong."

"Stay out of this. This is between me and her." Declan spun on Olivia as if waiting for an answer. "You went from leaving bed with me to having lunch with him?"

Sky's father stepped out of the kitchen and moved closer to them.

She'd given her virginity to him just hours ago, and here he stood insinuating she was a slut. The asshat. Olivia fought back the tears stinging the back of her eyes. Anger boiled beneath her skin all the way to the core as pain sliced her heart.

"Declan, you're right. I deserve better. A lot better than this." She rose and tossed her napkin on the table before glancing at Sky's father. "Mr. Love, can you handle the food?"

He nodded, and she turned to leave. Declan grabbed her arm, stopping her.

"Why are you playing these games? What the hell do you want from me?"

Trent broke Declan's hold and stood next to her as if protecting her from the big bad wolf. The rest of the men in the restaurant were watching with trained eyes. She'd never been more embarrassed in her life.

A tear slipped free. "There was a time when I just wanted you to love me." She gave a sad shake of her head. "Now...I don't want anything from you." She held his gaze, daring him to look away. "And you know that's the truth."

Olivia spun on her heels and ran out of the restaurant, not stopping until she stood in the middle of the parking lot. Her shoulders shook as fresh tears streamed down her face. She spun in place looking for her car. Too late it dawned on her that she'd ridden with Sky. Olivia crumpled, leaning against a car, cupping her face to hide her pain from the outside world.

"Jealousy will do it every time," Trent said from next to her. He reached down and lifted her up. He wrapped his arms around her, hugging her while the tears continued to fall.

She wiped her face and looked up at him. "I'm so sorry for ruining your lunch."

He gave her a sad smile. "You were the highlight of my lunch. You didn't ruin it. He did."

Her gaze flashed to the restaurant.

"Don't worry. The owner is having a heated discussion with him. He may be awhile."

"That's his dad."

"Yikes. Well, he deserves it. Is he always a douche?"

A chuckle bubbled from her lips. "He can be an ass, but he's never been...mean."

"Like I said, jealousy can do crazy things to men." He glanced around the parking lot. "Where's your car?"

"I didn't drive," she answered, wiping her tear-stained face. "The bride did before she rushed off."

Flynn strolled up, twirling his keys on his fingers. When he spotted Trent with Olivia, he quickened his step. "Trent."

"Flynn." Trent nodded.

His gaze met hers. The fine lines of his face deepened. "Olivia, what happened?

Where's Declan?"

Olivia shook her head and lowered her gaze.

"You mean the asshole that called her a slut because I sat down at her table?"

"I'll beat the shit out of him." Flynn's gaze flew to the door, and she could tell his intent by the fire in his eyes. She laid her palm on his arm. "Flynn, don't." Her voice was a whisper. The fire inside her had died. "Can you just please take me home? Sky had to leave, and I really don't want to call a cab."

"Of course." He wrapped his arm around her shoulder. "I'll beat the shit out of him later." He met Trent's gaze. "Thanks for taking care of her."

"My pleasure." He placed his palm on Olivia's arm. "You were right to walk away. You didn't deserve that."

She gave him a sad smile. "Thanks. I'm so sorry your meal was ruined."

Trent waved her worry away before Flynn led her back to his car.

7 CHAPTER

She'd holed up in her house for the rest of the week, being checked on by Sky and Flynn. Her heart was broken and shattered into a million pieces, but she masked her pain and reassured them she was all right. And the truth was, she would. Men didn't define her, and Declan's opinion...well, let's just say, her hopes of him being the man of her dreams were dwindling with each of his asshat reactions. He was honest when he said he didn't do relationships. His reaction proven it. Trust was more than an issue; it was the brick wall standing between them. He didn't trust her, no matter what asinine his reasoning was, and he'd given her zero reason to trust him.

Declan called a few times each day. Each attempt she let go to voice mail, not listening to what he had to say. She deleted the messages and tossed her phone back on the table. There were no words, no flowers, no pastry that could repair the humiliation he'd caused. It was becoming clearer and more evident that maybe...a relationship between them, just wasn't meant to be.

She opted out of Sunday lunch with the Loves, unable to face any of the family. By now the entire Love family knew what had transpired between them, and she didn't have the energy to put on a brave face. When Sunday night rolled around and Skylar and Alexis banged on her door, she opened it. They were dressed in little black dresses, their hair and makeup perfect, as though they were going out for a night on the town.

They shoved their way in. "Get dressed. We're going out."

"I'm not in the mood. You girls go and have a good time."

Sky nodded to Alexis, and they each took hold of one of her arms and dragged her to the bedroom.

"You have to go. This is my unofficial bachelorette party, and I need you with me." Skylar batted her long, thick black eyelashes. Alexis pushed out her fire engine red bottom lip.

Olivia glanced down at her night clothes. Last she'd looked, the bags beneath her eyes were enormous. "I'm not dressed, and I look like shit."

"We can fix that." Alexis clapped her hands. "Let me get my cosmetic trunk. We'll have you sexy as sin in no time at all."

"Yeah, because we all know how well that ended the last time you dolled me up."

Alexis tossed her arm around Olivia and squeezed. "This time is different. You'll be with us."

Olivia's stomach rolled at the thought of going out in public. She glanced at her comfortable bed and just wanted to get under the covers and forget the last week had happened.

"Oh, no you don't." Sky guided her to the bathroom. "Take a shower. It will wake your ass up. We'll wait."

Olivia walked into her bathroom and closed her door, leaning back on it. Her stomach rolled as she pushed off and started the shower. She didn't have a choice about going, not if it was Skylar's bachelorette party. Olivia just hoped not be the Debbie Downer of the group. She'd stay a few hours and then disappear into the night. It was her duty after all.

An hour later Olivia parked next to Alexis's car and closed the door, meeting them in front. She glanced around the parking lot of Double D, one of many island bars. The parking lot was empty except for a handful of cars and a few of the hotel busses that transported guests.

"Looks like it might be an early night." She pulled at the hem of her skirt that hugged her like a second skin.

Skylar glanced over her shoulder and grinned as she walked to the door. "Oh...I don't think so."

Dance music hit her in the face when Olivia followed Sky into the club. The thumping of the bass made her ears pop as she scanned all of the faces that had turned toward the door. "Tell me you didn't."

Skylar leaned in to talk in her ear. "I didn't, but Flynn did." She grinned and wrapped her arm around one of Olivia's arms, and Alexis took her other arm and leaned in to her ear.

"There's nothing wrong with some sexy football players."

"They needed a night off. It's not like I brought them here just for you."

Trent approached them with a beer in his hand. He held Olivia's gaze as he maneuvered through the crowd until he stood in front of her. "I know what this looks like..."

"Looks like a setup if you ask me." She glared at Skylar, who headed directly to the bar with Alexis in tow.

"Don't worry. I'll protect you from the others. We're all just here to have a good time and dance. Do you like to dance?"

His words weren't registering as she glanced around the room, feeling overwhelmed by the testosterone in the building.

"Olivia?"

When she didn't answer, he guided her by the elbow to an open table and took her purse and set it down before ushering her to the dance floor. Seconds later, Skylar and Alexis were by her side with drinks in their hands. Men surrounded the group as bodies moved to the fast-paced music.

Olivia pushed the fog from her mind and swayed to the music, letting the rhythm of the beat wash over her, lifting her mood. Trent's lips twisted into a smile.

She danced until sweat beaded her brow. The music continued, and Skylar and Alexis didn't look to be stopping anytime soon. Olivia pulled Sky to talk into her ear.

"I'm going to get some water and step out on the back deck for some air."

Skylar gave her two thumbs-up and continued to dance.

Trent followed her to the bar. She ordered water, and he got another beer before walking out onto the back deck. They leaned against the rail, staring out into the ocean. The brisk wind swept across her face, caressing her skin.

"My baby sister, Mia, is going to love it here."

Olivia smiled, inhaling the salty beach air. "Is she coming here on vacation?"

"Nah." He tipped the beer against his lips and swallowed. "She's a scientist. She works for Luke, and when he decided to set up shop, she was the first to sign up to move."

"The island has a lot to offer. It's beautiful."

Trent rested his elbow on the rail and linked his fingers together. "How are you holding up?" he asked nonchalantly as though they'd been friends forever.

"It's tiring." She glanced over her shoulder back into the club. "I try and keep a happy face for Sky and Flynn when I'm crushed inside. It's not their fault Declan lost his ever-lovin' mind."

He gave a slow nod before meeting her gaze. "It's going to take some time. I'm sure things will get easier. Has Declan called to apologize?"

She shrugged. "He's called. I just don't answer, and I delete his messages without listening to them. I have no idea if he's tried to apologize or is still calling me names."

Olivia took a swig of her water and swallowed around the lump in her throat to fight the tears forming in her eyes. "Let's take a walk."

She stepped down the stairs and kicked off her heels when she reached the sand. Trent matched his stride to hers as they headed down the beach.

"This is your town. Tell me something about it that I can tell Mia."

She tried for a smile at Trent's attempt to pull her from her thoughts. "Let's see. We have hot springs that not many people know about. There's zip lining, swimming with the dolphins, snorkeling, clubs." She gestured to the row of nightclubs. "We have land caves and underwater caves." She glanced up at him. "What does she like to do?"

"Work." His smile was genuine, as was the twinkle in his eyes. "She's a workaholic and has to be forced to get out of the house."

"Sounds familiar."

"She had a bad breakup a while back, and it took some of the shine from her eyes, but I'm thinking a place like this might lift her spirits."

Olivia moved to sit on one of the wooden beach chairs, careful not to flash him a glimpse of her panties when she sat. "You sound like a great big brother."

He shrugged. "We didn't have much growing up. Our parents died when I was eighteen and she was still a freshman in high school."

"And now you're this big-time football star."

He smiled. "I didn't think you knew who I was."

"I used to watch with Skylar's brothers." The thought of Declan made her heart ache.

He reached for her hand and squeezed. "Cheer up. It will all work itself out the way it was meant to be. Have faith in that."

He released her and clasped his hands on his stomach. "You know..." He glanced at her. "I don't have many women friends. Most of the women I meet are looking to date me or want me for my status and money." He smiled at her. "I'm glad we met. Even if your heart is taken, I enjoy your company."

She gave him a genuine smile. "Me too."

He rose and held out his hand to help her up. "We should probably head back."

She nodded and wiped the sand from the back of her dress.

"You know. If you ever just need to escape the island, you're more than welcome to come hang out with me in Boston." He pulled out his wallet and took a card from inside and handed it to her. "That's my address and my cell. You're welcome any time. I'm always on the road and hardly there, but if you need a place to escape, even when I'm not home, you're more than welcome."

"Thanks." She smiled and clutched the card as if it were her salvation. She just might have to take him up on that offer after the wedding.

"When is your team building over?"

"Next Sunday."

"I know this may sound strange, and I'd totally understand if you said no, but would you mind being my date to Skylar's wedding on Saturday? I don't think I can face her family alone, and I could use the moral support."

"Absolutely." He grinned and they walked back in easy banter. She'd laughed a few times, finding it easier to smile in Trent's company. They reached the steps back up to the club and he held out his arm for support while she dusted the sand from her feet before slipping on her shoes when they reached Double D.

8 CHAPTER

Declan set out the poker chips on the table. Flynn had almost turned around and walked out when Declan stopped him at the door. "I was wrong."

"You were more than wrong."

"I was an ass," Declan agreed.

Flynn let out a long sigh. "Declan man...you don't realize what you've done. You slept with her and knew she was a virgin and then called her a slut all in the same day. What the fuck is wrong with you?"

Declan ran his hand through his hair. He'd been asking himself the same question for a week. "I don't know. I saw her sitting with that guy, and I lost it. I thought she cared about me, but she doesn't, or she wouldn't have been on that date."

"So what? She's just supposed to sit around and wait for you to get your head out of your ass?"

"No, I didn't say that."

"That's what you implied." Flynn shook his head in disgust. "And for the record, that wasn't a date, you dipshit. He's a quarterback here for team building, and she was there doing a favor for Sky, testing the reception food since something happened to Skylar's wedding dress."

"Yeah well, they looked pretty cozy to me."

Flynn rolled his eyes. "Trent is a nice guy. He saw her eating alone and joined her. There is nothing going on between them. Well, there wasn't anything going on between them. Now..." He patted his brother's arm. "You screwed up, Declan. I wouldn't be surprised if more than one football player makes a pass at her tonight. It's not like you went out of your way to fix the problem."

Flynn had walked into Luke's and tossed his money down on the poker table.

Declan followed. "What do you mean tonight? Where is she?"

"Hate to break it to you, Dec, but you aren't her keeper."

"She's with Skylar and Alexis," Luke called out as he walked out of the kitchen holding two beers. He passed one to Declan.

"What's she doing with them? More wedding stuff?"

Luke stifled his grin. "I guess you could say that."

"Her bachelorette party," Flynn informed him. "And the entire Boston defensive line is at Double D's to make sure they all have a good time."

Declan clenched his jaw and his fist in an attempt to calm his anger.

Flynn patted him on the shoulder in passing. "Sorry, bro, but hell, you're not even dating. One quick lay sliding in her hot tight pussy and you've lost your mind?"

Declan's fist connected hard and fast with Flynn's jaw. The impact shoved him into the bar. Flynn righted himself, rubbing his jaw, and narrowed his eyes at his older brother.

Luke moved between them and held out his hands. "It's not Flynn's fault." He glanced at Declan. "This was Sky's idea, and I can't blame her." He turned to Declan. "We've been best friends almost all of our lives, and I've got to tell you, Declan, you crushed that poor girl when all she wanted from you was for you to love her. You broke her and destroyed her spirit, and Skylar and all of us will do anything necessary to give her back what you took away. She didn't deserve that." He shook his head. "Not from you, not when we all know that you care about her. You're just too damn stubborn to admit it."

"I asked her out." Declan's voice lowered in anger. "She said she had plans."

"To go to the movies," Flynn said while walking into the kitchen and grabbing an ice pack from the freezer. "That night she was going to the movies...by herself...because she didn't think you wanted more. She had it in her mind that you felt obligated to ask her out after sleeping with her."

"That's not why I asked her out."

Flynn shrugged, pressing the ice pack to his jaw. "Did you ask her before or after you slept with her?"

Declan clenched his jaw.

"Yeah, that's what I thought."

"Listen." Flynn picked up Declan's beer and handed it to him. "You need to figure out what the hell you want. If you're not sure, that's fine, take a step back, but don't play games with her."

"If you love her," Luke chimed in, "then don't let anything stop you from convincing her that you're the right man for her." Luke's gaze turned serious. "There's no greater feeling in the world that compares. Trust me."

Declan glanced at the poker table, and his stomach flipped. "I've got to go." He grabbed his keys and was out the door before either of them could ask where he was going. Hell, he didn't know where he was going.

****

Declan sat on Olivia's porch, his elbows on his knees and his head down, thinking of the right words to say, lost in thoughts of how he could possibly make things right. The sound of a car door shutting pulled him from his thoughts, and he looked up and met Olivia's gaze as she rounded the car. Her heartache was written all over her face.

She crossed her arms over her chest as she approached. "What are you doing here?"

Declan rose but didn't make a move to reach for her, even though all he really wanted to do was pull her into his arms and kiss away the hurt in her eyes. "You haven't answered my calls."

"You're a smart guy. I'm sure you can figure out why." She brushed past him and crossed her porch.

"Olivia..."

She paused with the key in her lock, her head lowered. "Go home, Declan." Her voice came out a whisper.

"I care about you."

She whipped around clenching her fist. "You don't get to say that. Not to me, not anymore."

He stepped up onto the porch. "It's true."

She shook her head. When a tear slipped free, she clenched her eyes closed. "Why are you doing this to me?"

Declan released a hesitant breath. "I don't want to lose you. I don't want to lose our chance to see if we work."

Her head snapped up to hold his gaze. "Too little too late."

Lie.

"You care about me. You can still feel the connection, the draw, between us."

She shook her head.

Lie.

He slowly advanced on her and raised his hand to cup her cheek. "I'm so sorry I hurt you."

Another tear slipped down her face, and she swiped it away. "You assumed the worst and practically called me a slut."

"I'm an asshole. Just ask Flynn."

She shook her head.

"You said you had plans, and then I saw you with...that guy. I thought you'd given up on me without even trying."

"Trent is just a friend." The words between them were a whisper.

"I know that now." He took her hands,

pleading with his eyes.

"Declan." She met his gaze. "You don't trust people. You don't ever let anyone in. I can't do this. I don't want to do this, not at arm's length." She cupped his face. "I'm sorry that I couldn't be that woman for you. The one you could trust with your heart."

Her shoulders shook as the tears began to fall.

The ice around his heart cracked, and he pulled her into his arms and held here close while she let out all of her frustrations through her tears. He stroked her hair and held her in the silence of the night. He kissed her forehead, letting his lips linger on her skin.

"Olivia...I do trust you. More than anyone, I trust you. I just lost my mind for a brief moment." She looked up at him through glassy, bloodshot eyes. "Let me make it right. Please, baby, don't give up on me."

"Declan..."

She began to shake her head when he cut off her protest, kissing her with all of the emotion he'd been holding back. He deepened the kiss, his palms on her waist. She twisted, opened the door, and they fell inside. He kicked the door closed and turned her, pressing her back against the door. She gave and he took as they both let the passion sizzling between them consume them once again. He broke the kiss, his heart beating wildly against his ribs. His shaft pressed painfully against his zipper.

"I'm sorry, Olivia." He stroked her cheek.

She held his gaze, searching his soul. "Don't let it happen again, Dec." She shook her head. "This is it."

He pressed his lips to hers as if in acknowledgment of her words. "We should slow down."

"Yeah, we should." She reached for his hand and pressed it against her thigh beneath her dress before pulling him by his collar to kiss her again. "We'll slow down later." She cupped him through his jeans. "Right now, I just want you."

She spread her legs, giving him easier access as his hand moved higher, teasing and stroking her wet thong beneath.

"You're wet." He breathed the words against her lips.

He moved the material and slipped his fingers over her folds, pulling a moan from her lips.

"Olivia...this isn't why I came over. I came to apologize."

"Shut up and kiss me."

"The room?"

"Here." Her chest heaved as he cupped her breast with his free hand.

He didn't have to be told twice. He

grabbed her panties and ripped. She inhaled a quick breath as he stroked her again. She was soaked.

"You like that?"

He grabbed the hem of her dress and yanked it off of her, tossing it at their feet. He reached between her legs again and slipped a finger inside. "Don't move."

Her channel clenched his finger. His demands turned her on. He pulled his finger free and stepped back, letting his gaze sweep over her. "Olivia, do you trust me?"

She hesitated, and he couldn't blame her.

"Olivia, I won't hurt you."

She nodded, and he took her hand and led her to the dining room table. He lifted her to sit on it and scooted her ass the edge. He slid his fingers back through her folds, making sure she wanted him, wanted this. He slowly kissed the column of her neck before moving to her breast, laving each of them until her nipples stood erect.

"Lie back," he demanded.

She was slow to reply.

"Olivia, lie back."

"What are you going to do?"

"Taste you," he answered. "Has anyone ever done this to you?"

She shook her head.

She eased onto her elbows. He kissed

a trail down her stomach while slipping a finger into her channel. She moaned. He ran his tongue down her torso, stopping before her mound. He held her gaze and moved lower, running his tongue over her slit. Her mouth parted on a gasp. If that turned her on, he was about to blow her mind.

He lifted her legs over his shoulder, and using his fingers to hold her open, he dove in. Stroking his tongue in and out of her, tasting and sucking her desire while holding her gaze. She was slow to blink.

"Breathe, Olivia."

A breath rushed free.

He used his fingers, inserting first one and then two while he stroked her nub with lazy circles with his tongue.

"Oh god." She closed her eyes.

"Watch me," he demanded, and her eyes popped open as she watched him with hooded eyes.

Her channel clenched around his fingers. She was close. So close. He grinned around his stroking and sucked her nub into his mouth. Holding it with his teeth, he pressed on it.

She moaned his name as her channel contracted, sucking his fingers farther in as her orgasm claimed her. He worked her until it passed, licking and tasting her on his tongue before he pulled free. She pushed herself to sit up as he popped the button on his jeans and shoved them and his boxers down. He stroked his cock, and her lusty gaze dropped to watch. He tossed the shirt off his body and yanked her body closer to him.

She met his gaze.

"Kiss me. I want you to taste how sweet you are."

She grabbed his head and pressed her lips to his as he held his cock at her entrance, rubbing it through her juices. He stilled, letting her taste herself. She moaned, sucking his tongue.

He broke the kiss. "Condom." He reached for his wallet, pulled out the package, and quickly covered himself before moving back into place. He slid in an inch. Her channel was still tight, even though she was slick.

She moaned and tossed her head back. He took her breast into his mouth, sucking while he held her still, and seated himself to the hilt. He held still until she opened her eyes and gave him a nod. He started moving in and out. She eased down to the table, and he lifted her legs over his arms, pulled her ass to the edge, and quickened his thrusts until her channel spasmed and she milked him dry. Her body was limp as he stayed seated inside her. He kicked off his shoes and his clothes and carried her into the bedroom. And again he made love to her, this time slow and not rushed. When they finished, he carried her into the bathroom and started the bath, and they soaked in the suds, letting all of the stress that had formed between them melt away.

He kissed her neck as she lay limp against his body. "Olivia?"

"Hmm?" Her eyes were closed as she answered.

He slid his fingers through hers and held her. "Let me take you out on a real date? The way I should have to begin with."

She opened her eyes and glanced up at him. "Okay." She turned in his arms and straddled his legs. "Declan, just so you know...this is it. If you hurt me again, I..."

He leaned forward and kissed her. "I'm not going to hurt you again." He leaned back. "I can't promise that I'll always do the right thing, or say the right words, but I'm willing to try....for you."

9 CHAPTER

Every five minutes for the last half-hour, Olivia had glanced at the clock as her nerves played havoc with her mind. Checking the mirror again, she added another coat of lip gloss to her lips. She didn't have a clue where he was taking her or if her sundress was acceptable attire. He'd called to tell her to dress casually, but that was it. Nothing about where they were going or what they were going to do. Anticipation coursed through her veins. She felt like a teen going on her first date. She held her gaze in the mirror and took a deep, relaxing breath.

"It's only, Declan. You know him," she said reassuringly.

She spotted the reflection of the night

stand in the mirror and hurried to grab some condoms and shove them in her purse. Turning off her bedroom light, she moved into the living room and paced across the floor, too nervous to sit down. She'd shifted the curtains to peer outside when she spotted his SUV pull in her driveway. She let the curtains fall back into place.

He knocked, and she counted to ten before opening, not wanting to seem too eager, even though she'd been waiting for what seemed an eternity.

Declan was standing at her door wearing a pair of jeans that hung low on his hips with a black tee-shirt stretched across his chest. The stubble of his five o'clock shadow had been shaved.

"These are for you." He held out a bouquet of daisies, her favorite flower, and she grinned.

"Thank you." She took them and kissed his cheek. "I never pegged you for a flower type of guy."

"I'm not," he replied.

She turned, leaving him to follow her into the kitchen. "I'm just going to put these in water."

She pulled the wilting roses from her date with the male escort out of the vase and tossed them in the garbage, replacing them with Declan's daisies. Declan silently watched her without question.

"So where are we going?"

"It's a surprise." He moved to stand behind her and pressed his lips to her neck. "You shouldn't have worn a dress." His palms landed on her thighs, and he inched his way up. "This might be too distracting."

She glanced over her shoulder and grinned. "I hear it's called foreplay."

A devastating handsome smile split his lips as he took her hand. "Food and talk first."

Grabbing her purse, she locked the door on the way out. Declan held the passenger door open for her and closed it behind her after she'd climbed in the car. If her nerves had been out of whack before, they were even more so now. This was a new side of Declan she'd never seen, the sweet side without a lot of gruff.

He slipped in the other side and started the engine before running his fingers through hers, resting their hands on her thigh.

She smiled at him. "How is it you're not working?"

"I've taken a long overdue vacation for the wedding." He lightly squeezed her hand. "And I'm glad I did."

He lifted their hooked fingers and kissed them.

They continued with nervous banter until he pulled into the marina and they got out of the car.

"What are we doing here?"

"I called in a favor." He led her down the dock, his large palm on the small of her back toward Luke's luxury yacht and helped her onboard.

Twinkle lights decorated the bow where a white tablecloth covered a small table. A candle was lit in the middle, and it was decorated with two place settings with crystal glassware. Silver domes covered the plates. Her heart skipped a beat as he pulled out her chair and waited for her to sit.

"Oh, Dec, it's beautiful."

He pressed an easy kiss to her neck. "You're beautiful."

Her cheeks warmed in response. When he took his seat, she leaned forward. "Does this seem weird to you? I mean don't get me wrong, but this doesn't seem like...you."

Declan cleared his throat before answering. "The guys suggested it. They didn't like my idea of dinner and a movie."

She slowly smiled. "Dinner and movie would have been perfect. I'm not high maintenance."

Declan's stiff exterior relaxed, helping to diminish her nerves. He lifted his lid and moved it aside, and she followed suit. The Italian aroma of garlic and tomato sauce drifted to her nose. Steam rose from her all-time favorite dish. "Lasagna is my favorite dish." She met his gaze. "How did you know?"

He popped the top on the wine bottle sitting in ice and poured them both a glass. "I pay attention. It's the only dish that you'll clean your plate when my mom makes it for Sunday lunch."

He'd noticed something so insignificant. All of this time, she wasn't even sure if he even knew she was at the table. "This looks just like your mom's."

"It should. She made it when I explained it was for you for our first date. I swear I heard her squeal with delight."

She picked up her fork and took a bite. Closing her eyes, she moaned at the flavor, taking her time to enjoy the bite. "I'm surprised you told your mom."

He paused with a bite lifted to his mouth. "She already knew. Both Sky and Flynn beat me to the punch."

"How does Flynn know?" Olivia picked up her wine glass and sipped.

Declan's gaze caressed her face. "I told him we were dating and you were off the market."

Olivia choked on the wine, using her napkin to swipe away the dribbles from her lips. "You what?"

Declan sat his fork down and rubbed his smooth chin. "Is there a problem being exclusive? Did you still want to date other people?"

Olivia rested her napkin on her lap. "No, but don't you think we should have discussed it before telling Flynn? This is our first date, and you just assumed..."

Declan held her gaze but remained silent. The delicious food was forgotten.

"I didn't assume, I hoped. There's a difference."

The tension in her body fizzled as she looked into his worried eyes. The emotion was uncharted territory for a man like Declan. He was always self-assured, decisive, and determined. He didn't know where they stood, and the thought endeared him to her.

"Okay, but next time...don't assume. I do have an opinion, whether you like it or not." She picked up her fork and took another bite.

He failed at hiding his smile. "I've known that for years."

She waved her fork in the air. "I know, I know, you're observant." She grinned. "Then you also know how I can get when I'm mad."

"Oh yeah. I've seen that too."

They finished their meal and retired to the padded seating area, where he took their wine and grabbed a blanket to cover her legs. They talked while stargazing and enjoying the late evening night. When she was in his arms, it felt right and natural, and they both started to relax as though they'd been together forever. She guessed in a way they had.

He drove her home and walked her to the door, stopping her before she walked inside by pulling her into his arms. He pressed his lips to hers, stroking his tongue, taking his time as he held her to his body. When he broke the kiss, his eyes sparkled.

"Thank you for tonight."

"Don't you want to come in?" She gestured with her thumb toward the door. "I can make us some coffee."

He sighed. "Do I want to? Yes. Am I going to? No. We both know what will happen if I go inside."

"I know." She grinned and rubbed circles on his bicep.

He ran his fingers through her hair, pushing the loose strands behind her ear. "I don't want to leave."

"Then don't." She drew him closer and kissed his collarbone.

"I'm trying to be a gentleman, Olivia, and you're not making it easy." He rested his palm on her cheek and ran his thumb across her lip.

"Why, when we've already..."

"I want to do this right."

"Uh, Declan, we're already past that."

"Olivia." He rested his forehead against hers. "I want this to be about more than sex. Not just for you, but for me too." He kissed her once more, and she watched him leave with the promise he'd see her tomorrow.

She went inside and leaned back against the door. Her brows dipped, and her heart fell into her stomach. Dating Declan was one thing, but the man who'd just walked her to the door wasn't Declan. He was a tame version of the man she wanted to be with. He was fooling himself. And damn it, she wanted the rough, gruff guy that she'd been dreaming of, not the timid, walking-on-eggshells version of the man.

10 CHAPTER

Sky shoved the hard hat on Olivia's head as they stared up at their new building. Their building was still in construction on the inside, but at least they now were getting the walls they needed. One step closer to being back in business. "Earth to Olivia."

Olivia adjusted her hat. "Sorry."

"How did it go last night?" Sky asked, stepping over a two-by-four laying in the entryway.

"He was sweet," she answered as they slowly made their way through the construction.

"Sweet? Are you sure you're talking about my brother?"

"I know, right?" Olivia linked her arm

around Sky's. "I mean, don't get me wrong, the night was nice, but it wasn't..."

"Declan."

"Yeah." She glanced at Sky. "You know."

Sky waved her arm. "I don't know what it is, but men turn weird when they're trying to impress us. It's like they grow another head, not realizing that we liked them before they pretended to be something they're not."

"Exactly."

"What are you going to do?"

Olivia shrugged. "What would you do?"

"That's easy. If it were me, I'd smack Luke on the back of the head...or...give him a reason to revert back to his old self."

"Seduction?" Olivia's brows rose.

"Worked the first time for you. I guess it depends on what you want to achieve. If it's sex, then hell yeah, buy some sexy lingerie and open the door with it on. I guess it depends on what you're after."

"I want to date the Declan I know."

"The mean, gruff, a bit of a pain in the ass, call-you-out guy that you know? It makes sense."

"Enough about me. What time are we all showing up at the hotel on Saturday to get ready for the wedding?"

"We have all day reservations at the hotel spa. The complete package, hair, nails, massages complete with champagne and lunch since the wedding starts at dusk."

"Perfect." She nudged Sky's shoulder as they made their way out of the building. "I still can't believe you're getting married."

Skylar's eyes sparkled. "I love him. I can't imagine my life without him."

"I'm so happy for you."

"Do you have plans with Declan tonight?"

"Yeah. I offered to cook dinner. Now I'm thinking we're only going to need some whipped cream."

"You're so bad." Sky chuckled.

"I'm trying," Olivia answered.

****

Olivia skipped on the lingerie and whipped cream she'd planned. Instead, she intended to face Declan head-on. Their dinner was in the oven to stay warm when he arrived.

"Can I get you something? Beer, wine, water, tea?"

"Tea, please."

Olivia poured him a tea before picking up her wine. She tilted her head, silently studying him while trying to find the right words. "Can I tell you something without you taking it the wrong way?"

"Sure." His brows creased.

"I've known you most of my life. I'm used to your gruff, don't-take-any-shit attitude. I've watched you pick on your sister in one breath and defend her with your next. You're loyal, you're caring, and to the point, I love that about you..." She licked her lips, debating if she should continue. "I liked that man, not the one that has moonlight dinners on a yacht and flowers and leaves me at my door. I'm not comfortable with him."

Silence lingered between them as he searched her gaze, piercing her and holding her in place. "Is that right?"

She nodded. "Yeah."

"Good, I'm glad you think so." He put his tea down, closed the distance between them, and picked her up, heading for the bedroom. "You deserve better. You know that, right?"

"I want you, Declan, the real you."

Declan kicked the door closed with his boot before easing her down onto the bed. "Dinner's going to have to wait. I want my dessert first. You want the real me, sweetheart? You've got it."

He tossed his shirt over his head and dropped it on the floor before reaching for her buttons, making haste to divest her of her clothing. Her heartbeat quickened, and her insides quivered when he touched her as he spent an hour delivering on his promise. He'd driven her to the brink before easing away, over and over again, until she was begging him to send her over the edge, and he'd finally done just that.

Olivia and Declan relaxed with easy banter while they ate their meal. They put in a chick flick and cuddled on the couch well into the night, and each night up until Friday night.

Olivia swallowed around the lump in her throat when Declan knocked on her door. She pulled him in and led him to the couch to sit. "I need to tell you something, and I need you to keep your cool."

"That doesn't sound good." He exhaled a deep breath. "Lay it on me."

She pressed her lips together and swallowed. "I have a date for the wedding." She was quick to continue. "He's just a friend. There's no chemistry, and he knows it. I asked him the night of Skylar's party."

Declan sat forward in the chair and rubbed his hand over his head. "Who?"

She chewed her lip. "Trent. The guy from the restaurant. He's just a friend."

Declan jumped to his feet and started pacing the living room. "Can you cancel?"

Olivia's shoulders dropped. "No. That's rude." She walked over to him and pressed her hands on his chest. "I'm with you. You know that, right?"

He nodded and held her gaze. His eyes

troubled.

"He knows my heart is yours. He's just a friend. Someone I trust who was going to help me get through a difficult time when we were on the outs."

"You've only known him two weeks. How can you trust him?"

She shrugged. "I don't know. I just do. He's never made a pass at me, not once. Flynn knows him."

"That doesn't help his cause," Declan grumbled.

She stepped back. "Do you trust me?"

He pulled her into his arms and held her. "Yes." He glanced down at her. "But you need to tell him that I'll be tagging along."

She chuckled. "That's a great idea. You two can get to know each other."

"Great." His reply dripped with sarcasm.

The rest of their evening was just as she'd imagined. Declan no longer tried to impress her. They'd eaten and watched a movie before falling asleep on the couch and waking several hours later. He kissed her and carried her to bed before leaving her house.

The rest of the week was split between last-minute wedding stuff that she helped Sky with and spending time with Declan. His house, hers, and just really getting comfortable in their new situation.

****

Olivia slammed her palm down on the alarm clock and slowly opened her eyes. Today was Skylar's wedding. Olivia smiled as she rolled out of the bed and headed for the shower.

She turned the water nozzles on and let the water run, wiping the sleep from her eyes in the mirror. She glanced through the reflection at her empty shampoo bottle, remembering to toss it away. She'd opened the sink cabinet to grab another bottle when her heart froze. The package blocking the bottle made her heart drop into her stomach. Her mind raced as she remembered what day it was. Her heart sank as she realized that she'd missed her monthly friend, Flo.

She clenched her eyes and rose without grabbing the shampoo. She moved to sit on the commode and buried her head in her hands. "This isn't happening. I must have the date wrong."

She left the bathroom and headed into the kitchen, where she had a calendar hanging on the inside of one of her cabinets. She opened it and stared at the little circle that confirmed she was indeed late. Her feet felt as if they were encased in concrete as she stared at the numbers on the calendar. She rested her hand on her stomach and closed her eyes, shaking the unimaginable thought from her mind.

Her phone rang, startling her back into the present. She answered, resting it against her ear.

"Hello."

"I didn't wake you, did I?" Sky asked.

"No..." Her voice trailed off.

"Olivia, what's wrong?"

"Nothing." Olivia shook the thoughts from her head. Her best friend didn't need this on the happiest day of her life. She shut the cabinet door and headed back into her room. "I was just about to get in the shower. Are we still meeting at the spa in an hour?"

"Are you sure you're okay? Is Declan there?"

"No. He didn't stay last night. I'm fine, really." She swallowed around the lump in her throat. "Enough about me, what about you? Are you nervous yet?"

"Not nervous at all. Luke and I were meant to be together. We're just making it official."

Olivia smiled. "I'm getting in the shower, and I'll meet you there."

There was hesitation in Skylar's voice. "Olivia...are you sure you're all right?"

"Yeah," she said, trying to convince herself and Skylar. "I'm good. You're getting married today," Olivia squealed into the phone. "I'll see you in an hour."

Olivia got Skylar off the phone without any more prodding. Olivia pushed all baby worries to the back of her mind as she showered and hurried through her routine so she wouldn't be late meeting Skylar.

11 CHAPTER

Arriving at the spa, she was escorted back where Skylar and Alexis were waiting, already wearing white robes and fluffy flip-flops. Each had a glass of champagne as they smiled and talked.

"I thought I was going to have to send out a search and rescue," Skylar teased.

"Sorry. I had to run an errand first."

"Do tell." Alexis handed Olivia a glass of champagne. "Did you and Declan have a quickie?"

Blood drained from Olivia's face as she sat down in one of the plush chairs. Her gaze dropped to the floor as she tried, yet again, to process how her missing period might throw her and Declan's life into shambles.

Skylar and Alexis squatted in front of her. They each took a hand.

"What's wrong? And don't tell me nothing. I can see it in your eyes. Talk to us, Olivia," Skylar demanded.

Olivia opened her purse, pulled out the drugstore bag, and handed it to Skylar.

Skylar dumped the pregnancy test out of the bag, and her eyes widened. "You don't think?"

She shrugged and met her gaze. "I'm late." Her words came out a whisper. "And I'm never late."

"Oh, honey." Skylar shoved the box back inside. "You're probably late due to stress. How many days late?"

Olivia's heart clenched. "Two weeks."

Alexis rose. "It's probably still too early to tell. You and Declan only sealed the deed about three weeks ago. You should wait another week and then take the test."

"Have you told Declan?" Sky asked.

The last thing Olivia wanted to do was to tell Declan when she wasn't sure herself. They both knew it was a possibility. She swallowed around the lump in her throat. "No."

Her gaze shifted between both women. Apprehension filled her veins. "Please don't say anything. I don't want to freak him out. Not today."

Olivia rose. "Forget I said anything." She pasted a smile on her face while wrapping her arm around Sky's. She nudged her shoulder. "Now tell me where I can get one of those fancy robes."

She tried her best to stay in the moment, not letting the things she couldn't control eat at her mind. They spent the afternoon being pampered in preparation for the wedding. Hour later, they were in the bridal room, every one dressed as family members came and went to wish Skylar good luck and tell her how beautiful she looked.

Declan was the last to walk into Skylar's room. He smiled and kissed his sister's cheek. "You look beautiful."

"Thanks, Declan." She squeezed his hand.

"You know you can still back out."

Skylar shook her head. "Fat chance. I've waited for this day my whole life."

Declan moved to Olivia and cupped her cheek. "I'll see you later?"

She nodded, afraid to answer for fear he'd recognize the trepidation in her voice.

Declan glanced one last time at Sky and nodded before he left the room. Olivia released her pent-up breath, knowing it was just a matter of time before she knew for sure that she'd single-handedly ruined Declan's life. He wasn't ready to be a father, and if she was honest, she wasn't ready to be a mother.

****

Olivia straightened Skylar's train before moving to take her place in line. Declan met her at the door and held out his arm. He smiled at her as she rested her hand in the crook of his arm. They both exhaled a deep breath and smiled before heading out the double doors. They followed the path to where the wedding was set up looking out over the beach as the sunset dipped behind the horizon. Flowers lined the chairs and the arch where the preacher and Luke patiently waited. Flynn and Alexis walked slowly in front of them. Declan's mother and other brothers were already seated on the bride's side.

Sky deserved this. She deserved every bit of happiness that her future held. She'd been the unstoppable force behind everything in her life, even their friendship in the third grade. The little girl back then had walked into the classroom as though she'd owned the place and pointed at Olivia before announcing that they would be best friends forever. It wasn't until later that Skylar had told her that, even though she'd not known a thing about her at the time, it was her energy she'd thought the prettiest.

Olivia smiled, her heart full for her best friend. Declan released her to stand on the podium before the wedding march queued up. Every eye turned on the door where Skylar stood clutching her father's arm. Tears of joy clouded Olivia's eyes. This was how it was meant to be. Skylar had fought for what she wanted, never giving up. This was how it was supposed to be. This was how her own life should be. Olivia shifted her gaze to Declan to find him watching her and not Skylar's approach, his normal hard emotions now soft and reflecting in his eyes. There was a longing in his eyes. Their lives were about to change and he didn't even know it. A baby? The thought once terrified her, wasn't so scary now. She'd always wanted to be a mom, even if the married soul mate didn't come until later. A baby. She grinned.

Skylar handed Olivia the bouquet before taking Luke's hands, and there was nothing Olivia could do to pull her gaze away from Declan's. It was as if he held her wrapped in magic. Heat flooded her cheeks as the cheering in the crowd sounded. She broke Declan's hold and turned to find Skylar bent over Luke's arm in a kiss that said "finally" for both of them.

****

If the awkwardness of thinking she

might be pregnant wasn't stressful enough at the reception, she sat at the round table with Declan on one side of her and Trent on the other. The tension between them was thick enough to slice with knife.

Trent reached across the table and held out his hand. "No hard feelings?"

Declan shook his hand. "Not as long as you know she's with me."

Trent smiled with a slight nod as he rose. "I'm going to grab a beer from the bar. Can I get you two anything?"

"No thanks." Olivia gave him a small smile and rested her hand on her stomach as she watched Trent leave.

Declan cleared his throat. "Do you want to tell me now what's wrong?"

"Nothing." She tried to smile.

Lie.

"Olivia, I know you aren't telling the truth." Declan nodded toward the bar. "Is it Trent? Are you uncomfortable?"

She didn't answer, knowing that if she did and told him no, he'd know she was lying. So she countered with the truth instead. "Declan." She cleared her throat and moved her chair closer to him to whisper, "I didn't want to tell you here, but I'm late."

"Late for what?" His brows dipped in confusion, and her cheeks heated.

"My monthly visitor." His eyes widened, and his mouth parted. Not quite the response she was looking for, but she could hardly blame him. "Say something."

"If you are, we'll deal with it."

Their conversation was cut short when Trent returned to the table. His gaze shifted between both of them. "Am I interrupting?"

Olivia's heart squeezed as Declan stood. "I think I'm going to need that drink now."

He turned and walked away, and Olivia closed her eyes. The butterflies in her belly fell like concrete weights sitting in her stomach.

"Don't tell me you guys got in a fight in the three minutes I was gone?"

She lifted her gaze to Trent's. "Not quite." She clasped her hands and held them in her lap. "I kind of dropped a bombshell on him..."

Trent's gaze flew to the bar where Declan was throwing back a shot.

"Must have been a doozey. I wasn't expecting him to let you out of his sight with me around."

"You can say that." She cleared her throat and shook her thoughts. "I'm sorry. I'm not being very good company tonight."

He shrugged. "Not a big deal. I'm enjoying having a break from the guys." His look turned serious. "You remember what I said about visiting Boston?"

She nodded.

"The offer still stands." He glanced over his shoulder at Declan getting a refill of his drink.

"Thanks," she answered, her gaze on Sky as she approached Declan at the bar. His face was scrunched, and Sky's eyes narrowed on him. She pointed in Olivia's direction.

"Excuse me a moment," she mumbled and rose, heading to the bar to stop the sibling argument she knew was about her.

She stepped up behind Declan.

"Sky, I'm not ready to be a father."

Olivia was afraid to move, afraid to breathe, thinking that they might turn around and see that she'd overheard. Her heart crumbled. They turned toward her.

"Olivia, he didn't mean it," Sky said.

Olivia fought the tears in her eyes when Declan remained silent.

She swallowed around the lump in her throat and pulled Sky in for a hug. "I'm so happy for you. But I'm not feeling too well. I hope you don't mind..."

"Don't you dare let him run you off."

"Olivia, let me explain." Declan turned to face her.

"No need." She let out the breath she'd been holding. Bile rose into Olivia's throat. "Excuse me."

She spun on her heels, headed back to the table, and grabbed her purse. Trent rose in response. "What happened? What did he do?"

"I need to go." She looked up into his eyes. "You're more than welcome to stay, but I need to go."

"I'm only here for you." He took her elbow and guided her toward the exit while Flynn, Skylar, and Luke were busy talking to Declan.

"I think I'll take you up on that offer." She glanced up at him. "Can we leave today?"

"Of course." His brows dipped as he led her through the hotel. "I just need to grab my things." He gave her a worried look. "I'll meet you at the ferry in twenty minutes. Is that too soon?"

She shook her head. "The sooner, the better."

12 CHAPTER

Skylar smacked Declan in the back of the head. "Are you kidding me? How could you say that?"

"I didn't know she was standing right there." Declan folded his arms over his chest. "Olivia caught me off guard. I mean I knew it was a possibility because the condom broke, but...I...we...didn't know. I'm still in shock."

Flynn gripped the bar, leaning against it. "Did you say anything at all when she told you?"

"I told her we'd deal with it."

Flynn narrowed his eyes. "Could you be any more insensitive?"

"Declan. She's probably scared and needed your support. I can't believe your reaction to a possible pregnancy was that you'd deal with it."

"Olivia left." Skylar's father stood

behind them with his arms crossed, a look of disappointment in his eyes, which he directed at Declan. "And after hearing why, I can't say I blame her."

Martin Love ushered the others back to the party and the guests before tossing his arm around his son's shoulders and leading them somewhere private they could talk. They walked toward the pool area and sat under one of the umbrella tables.

"Dad..."

"Declan." He held up his hand. "Let me speak."

Declan leaned back in his chair and pressed his lips together.

"I'm sure you're confused right now, but let me give you a little advice because your next actions might just define the rest of your life."

Declan remained silent.

"I have no doubt that you'd step up and be a good father, in the event she is pregnant, and I think, deep down, she already knows that. What you have to think about is how you feel about Olivia. Not Olivia, the potential mother of your child, or Olivia, your sister's best friend. But Olivia, the woman." His dad stood. "If you love her, you need to act now and let her know you care. If you don't..." He shrugged. "The family will still love her and support you and her in whatever you two need. This is a defining moment in your life." He clasped his son's shoulder. "I guess there's only one question left to ask yourself, and only you know the answer to that."

His dad left him sitting at the table.

Did he love her? Yeah, he did. He stood from the table, unbuttoned his jacket, and slid it off his shoulders before pulling his keys out of his pocket. He quickened his gait as he headed through the hotel to try and catch her, only stopping when he ran into Trent checking out.

"Where is she?"

Trent shoved his credit card back into his wallet and let out a long breath as he turned to face Declan. "Why is it every time I see you and her together she's upset? You know I should really be thanking you." He shoved his wallet in his pocket. "I didn't have to win her over. Just had to catch her when she fell."

Declan clenched his fist and stepped up into Trent's face. His eyes narrowed in challenge.

Trent's lips twitched. "Have a nice life, Declan." He winked. "I know we will."

Trent grabbed his bags and stepped around Declan as he whistled.

Declan grabbed onto Trent's arm and spun him around, his fist instantly connecting with Trent's jaw.

Trent rubbed the red mark while his smile grew. "I couldn't have planned that better. You just nailed your coffin shut." He winked. "Whose side do you think she'll be on now?"

Declan stormed out of the hotel and toward his car. He had to find Olivia and talk some damn sense into her.

****

Trent rubbed his throbbing jaw. Declan landed a mean punch when pissed off. Flynn strolled over to the counter. "You're a better actor than I thought."

Trent grinned. "He wasn't hard to provoke. He already loves her. It's like you said. He just needed a swift kick in the ass."

"I couldn't have said it better myself." Flynn patted his shoulder. "So what are you going to do now?"

Trent shrugged. "Go to the ferry and see if she shows up. If she does, then I'll take her to my place and let her cool off for a few days while she gets her head on straight and figures out what she wants to do."

"Jealously is a fickle bitch. I hope Declan doesn't screw this up."

"You and me both."

"I owe you." Flynn folded his arms across his chest and watched as Declan sped by the front door on the way out of the parking lot.

"I'll collect when Mia moves here. You can keep her out of trouble."

"Of course," Flynn answered. "How hard could it be?"

Trent chuckled. "You haven't met my sister. Trouble is her middle name. She can attract slime balls from a mile away."

Trent shook Flynn's hand before walking out of the hotel. The plan they'd concocted had easily worked. The rest was up to the lovebirds.

****

Olivia swiped away the last tears she'd cry over Declan Love. Her heart clenched just thinking his name. She shoved a couple shirts into her bag and was grabbing some jeans when she heard the knock on her door. She folded them as she went to the door. She opened it to find Declan on her stoop and, with a flick of the wrist, shut the door just as fast.

"Go away, Declan."

Anger seethed in her soul, wrapping around her and taking hold.

Her door opened, and she continued to her room. She shoved the jeans into her bag. "You aren't welcome here."

"Olivia, you have to listen."

She spun on him. "I don't have to do a

damn thing." She pointed toward the door. "Now leave."

He closed the distance between them and rested his palms on her arms. Fire licked her veins.

"You didn't let me explain."

"What's to explain?" She swiped his hands from her arms and went back into the closet to grab more clothes. "You're not ready to be a father."

"You don't even know if you're pregnant." He watched every move she made like a hawk.

She dropped a shirt into the bag and lowered her head. It was true. She didn't know if she was, but at least she knew where he stood on the matter. She glanced up at him as tears clouded her eyes. "If I am...I'll do this by myself."

"Would you let me explain?" He guided her to the bed to sit while he knelt in front of her and took her hands. "I said I wasn't ready to be a father. I wouldn't even know where to begin. Not that I didn't want to be." He searched her eyes. "I love you, Olivia."

A tear broke free, leaving a wet path down her cheek. She swiped it away.

"You're only saying that because of the situation. You don't mean it."

He cupped her cheeks. "I've never meant anything more....ever."

She stood and walked into her

bathroom, grabbing her toiletries. "I don't have your gift of knowing whether you're telling the truth, Declan. All I have is your actions." She tossed the items into the bag and zipped it up. "And right now, all your actions prove to me is that you're trying your best to get me to stay. If you'd told me a week ago that you loved me, before all of this, I might have believed you."

"Damn it, Olivia, I'm telling you the truth. Baby or not, I love you."

She picked up her bag and rested the strap over her shoulder. "I have to go."

"Please, Olivia, I need you."

A tear slipped free. "This isn't about you." She adjusted the strap on her shoulder. "This is about doing what's right for me. And right now, I need time to think."

"You can think here." He held up his hands in surrender. "I won't bother you. Just please don't go with Trent."

Realization dawned on her. That was his reason for being there and asking her to stay. He'd figured out her plans. "How did you know?"

"I ran into him in the lobby. He was gloating that he'd won."

"Is that why you're here?" Her eyes searched his.

"No. Yes. What does it matter? I love you. Isn't that enough? I'm not just telling you what you want to hear."

"Why do you love me? I mean what is it about me that you love?"

"What?" Confusion clouded his face.

"Give me one reason why you love me."

He paused too long.

"Answering that shouldn't be so hard." She swallowed around the lump in her throat. "Forgive me if I don't believe the words. You only show up when you don't get your way. It's like you don't want me, but you don't want anyone else to have me either." Her words were a whisper. "You can't have it both ways. Goodbye, Declan."

She spun on her heels and left him standing in her room. Once out of her house, she threw her bag into the passenger seat, got in the car, and backed out of the driveway.

Tears clouded her vision as she drove toward the ferry as her mind replayed their conversation over and over in her mind. She parked her car and watched as people boarded the ferry. Trent was standing on the dock and held her gaze. When she didn't move to get out of the car, he gave her a slight nod and turned, leaving her behind. She watched the ferry as it pulled away from the landing and slowly moved across the water. She closed her eyes, grasping the wheel tight as her shoulders shook and the tears flowed free.

Her door opened, and Declan pulled her out and into his arms, holding her tight.

"I never meant to hurt you, baby."

She grasped his shirt as the tears continued.

"I'll call the ferry back. You can still go."

She shook her head and leaned out of his hold, wiping the tears. "I didn't miss the ferry."

He guided her over to one of the picnic tables and eased her down onto the wooden bench.

"You asked me why I love you."

All the fight left her body. She didn't want to do this again. She didn't have the energy. "Declan..."

"No." He squatted in front of her. "Let me answer." He cleared his throat. "I love you because you're beautiful. You're funny, and you have a huge heart. You love my sister and my family as much as I do. I love you because you make me laugh and you drive me nuts. I love you because you're you. I didn't know how to answer that before, not because I didn't love you, but because there are so many reasons why I do." He cupped her cheek. "I couldn't pick just one."

Olivia licked her lips as she held his gaze, trying her best to tell if he meant his words. Her mind reeled from his declaration.

Declan dropped to his knee and took

her hand. "Marry me."

Her mouth parted. "Declan, we don't know if I'm pregnant."

"That's why I'm asking now. I don't want you to ever question if I mean it. All of our relationship you thought I was reactive to our circumstances, even when that wasn't the reason for my actions. I NEVER want you to doubt this moment. I'll love you with all of my heart, Olivia. I always will. Please do me the honor of being my wife."

"You're serious?"

"Have you known me to be any other way?"

She moved to stand and put some space between them, forming the letter T with her hands. "I think we need an emotional time-out. You're not thinking clearly."

He watched every movement she made. "I am thinking clearly. More than I have ever."

She shook her head and held up her hand, stopping him from stepping forward. "I won't let you do this." She walked to her car and opened the door. "If you want to marry me, I mean really marry me, you won't ask when I'm upset. You'll wait until the right time." She gestured around. "This isn't the right place or the right time."

13 CHAPTER

Two weeks later. Skylar and Olivia strolled on Main Street, keeping their Sunday ritual of window-shopping for things to restock the store.

"Did you take the test?" Skylar linked her arm with Olivia's.

"Yep," she answered.

"And?"

Olivia shook her head. "And...I want Declan to be the first to know."

"Are you telling him today?" Sky asked as they headed for her car.

"Yeah. I'm going to pull him aside at your parents' after lunch."

They got into Sky's car and headed to her parents' house. "Have you seen him since the wedding?"

Declan had made a point of calling her during the day and stopping by her house when he wasn't at work. Their relationship had eased, the tension gone. The last time they'd made love, he'd run his hand over her belly and placed tiny kisses on her skin. "Everyday."

"And?" Sky glanced at her. "Still sparks?"

Olivia nodded. She'd never lost the sparks for Declan. "Yeah. He's being himself."

"You mean an ass?"

Olivia grinned. "No." She glanced at Sky. "He's really trying. You know? He goes out of his way to make me feel loved and cherished. I just hope it's not because he's worried."

Sky parked the car behind the SUVs in front of her parents' house. Music was playing in the backyard. "Five bucks says your parents are dancing."

"I'm sure they are," Luke said, walking up behind them. He kissed Skylar and smacked her ass as she walked in front of them. "You guys are in for a treat. I hear we have guests." He wiggled his brows and winked.

Sky exchanged a confused look with Olivia.

They walked into the backyard and rounded the house. Olivia grinned as she scanned the yard. The complete Boston defensive line stood in the backyard. Her smile grew as they all turned to face her. "You guys. What are you doing here?"

Trent raised his beer in her direction. "We couldn't miss this."

"Miss what?" she asked as she and Sky moved farther into the yard.

The line of men parted, and Declan stepped forward, holding wilted daisies and dressed in a suit and tie. Sky gasped, and Olivia's smile slipped. She gave a quick shake of her head. He wasn't about to do this. Here. Oh god.

He stepped toward her and took her hand. "Olivia."

"You don't have to do this," she whispered, hoping only he would hear.

"Yes I do." He dropped to his knee, pulled out a box, and flipped it open.

"No, no, no." She yanked him up by his arm and pulled him farther away from the crowd. "No you don't." She whispered between them. "I'm not pregnant."

Understanding dawned on him, and the confusion in his face cleared, and he pulled her back closer to the others.

"I love you. Not because of what you aren't..." he glanced to her belly to make sure she understood exactly what she was saying. "...but because of who you are." He kneeled in front of her again. "I told you I loved you, and this is the right time." He glanced behind him. "The right place with the right people to witness. Marry me."

She could feel the love flowing from him. It was in his eyes, in his gestures, and everything she'd hoped and dreamed. Her eyes glassed over as she nodded.

He smiled and slipped the ring on her finger before standing up and devouring her lips with his in a sensual kiss that made her blush.

"Finally," Flynn called out, making the teary-eyed group laugh.

****

Two weeks later in Vegas, with both of their best friends present, Olivia and Declan made their vows to each other in front of friends and the Elvis lookalike in the little white chapel. If it had been up to Declan, they would have just done the drive-thru service and headed straight back to the hotel. They'd both nixed the idea of planning a wedding and having to deal with the trials that Olivia had witnessed from Sky's grand affair. Declan broke the kiss, and his eyes softened as love flowed from him to her.

"My wife." He grinned. "I'll love you forever."

"And I'll always love you back."

Truth.

She smiled and pulled him in for another kiss.

DECLAN

Text KATE to 313131 and get a text message on release dates or go to her website at <u>www.kateallenton.com</u> and sign up for her newsletter!

Other Books by Kate Allenton

Suggested Reading Order

REDEMPTION (Book 5)
CHANCE ENCOUNTERS (Book 6)
DESTINED HEARTS (Book 7)

PHANTOM PROTECTORS BOX SET (Books 1-4 in one bundle, 964 pages)
RECKLESS ABANDON (Book 1)
BETRAYAL (Book 2)
UNTAMED (Book 3)
GUIDED LOYALTY (Book 4)

CARRINGTON-HILL INVESTIGATIONS
DECEPTION (Book 1)
DEADLY DESIRE (Book 2)

SHIFTER PARADISE BOX SET
NOT MY SHIFTER/ SINFULLY CURSED

KARMA

SOPHIE MASTERSON SERIES/ DIXON SECURITY
LIFTING THE VEIL (Book 1)
BEYOND THE VEIL (Book 2)
VEILED INTENTIONS (Book 3)
VEILED THREATS (Book 4)

HELL BOUND
MYSTIC TIDES BOX SET

LOVE SERIES
SKYLAR
DECLAN

FLYNN (COMING SOON)
REED (COMING SOON)
LANDON (COMING SOON)
ALEXIS (COMING SOON)
TANNER (COMING SOON)
GABE (COMING SOON)
JACKSON (COMING SOON)

ABOUT THE AUTHOR

Kate has lived in Florida for most of her entire life. She enjoys a quiet life with her husband, Michael and two kids.

Kate has pulled all-nighters finishing her favorite books and also writing them. She says she'll sleep when she's dead or when her muse stops singing off key.

She loves creating worlds full of suspense, secrets, hunky men, kick ass heroines, steamy sex and oh yeah the love of a lifetime. Not to mention an occasional ghost and other supernatural talents thrown into the mix.